Designing Love
Book 1

I0523652

Baby
by **Design**

ELLEY ARDEN
Author of *Crashing the Congressman's Wedding*

C R I M S O N
R O M A N C E

F+W Media, Inc.

This edition published by
Crimson Romance
an imprint of F+W Media, Inc.
10151 Carver Road, Suite 200
Blue Ash, Ohio 45242
www.crimsonromance.com

ISBN 10: 1-4405-7093-0
ISBN 13: 978-1-4405-7093-3
eISBN 10: 1-4405-7094-9
eISBN 13: 978-1-4405-7094-0

Acknowledgments

First and foremost, I have to acknowledge my editor, Barb Wilson. She makes me feel like a rock star when I know I'm anything but.

I also couldn't have written a book like this without intimate knowledge of a big, loud, loving Italian-American family. I'm truly blessed, and I love you all.

And finally, ovarian cancer left a hole in my life and my heart when it claimed my grandmother. In an effort to do my part to make sure future generations can avoid a similar pain, I'll be donating a portion of proceeds from this book to the Ovarian Cancer Research Fund.

For Gigi, who would've been leery of Tony, too...
until she saw him in a suit.
And for Gramma Reet, who taught me the greatest show of love is
a good, hard cheek pinching.
How'd a girl get so lucky to have grandmothers like you?

CHAPTER ONE

"My God, he cleans up nice." Trish DeVign said the words around a mouthful of anise-flavored birthday cake while she stared at a suit-and-tie clad Tony Corcarelli. His colorful tattoos were covered by the sleeves of a fitted single-breasted jacket and navy dress shirt. His pitch-black hair was combed away from his face. And he'd shaved, leaving a slight contrast of color on his cheeks and chin, drawing her eyes straight to his unblemished lips.

"Too bad he's such a screw up."

Trish tore her gaze from Tony to level her best friend with the stink eye. "That's not a nice thing to say about your brother."

"It's true. Look at him playing paper football with the kids while he's dressed in an $800 suit. He should try spending less on clothes, keeping more of that money in the bank, and acting like a grown-up once in a while."

Trish sighed as the sinfully handsome man flicked a white triangle across the table to the tune of children's cackles. "I think it's cute."

"You would. Shoot. Aunt Helen's got a slice of cake big enough to prompt diabetic shock. Where's my mother?" Angie whipped her head in all directions and growled. "I'll be back."

Alone in the midst of familial chaos, Trish tapped her nails on the bottom of her plate and looked around the banquet room of Cestone's Italian Restaurant. Four generations of Corcarellis were a sight to be seen; a sight that made her smile even though it made her heart hurt. In the corner of the room, middle-aged women fussed over the food tables, directing servers, corralling cookies, and spearing meatballs, while in the center of the room, middle-aged men ate until their belt buckles popped. All around, the older generation talked...and talked...and talked, punctuating every sentence with nodding heads and waving hands. She loved them all, but it was the children that tethered her heart, tugging her toward their joyful noises.

"Tony, me next. I'll kick your as…"

Trish surmised the kid to be about twelve, and when he noticed her approaching, he bit off his last word amid oohs and ahhs from other kids around the table.

With sheepish eyes he looked from her to his cousin. "I'll beat you is all. That's what I was gonna say, Tony. Honestly."

"Sure you were," Tony said with a grin that tightened the tether on Trish's heart. "Just gimme ten minutes to throw some cake down my throat and I'm all yours." He stood, smoothed a hand down the button line of his suit coat, and blinded her with the full power of his male magnetism. All it took was a crooked smile, one that created a dark dip in his left cheek, not quite a dimple—no, dimples were too cute for a man this…edgy. "Hey, Boss Lady. I'd ask you to join me for cake, but I see you beat me to it."

Trish looked down at her empty plate and swallowed the ridiculous butterflies that escaped their netting whenever Tony came around. "What can I say? It was delicious."

He grinned again. "In that case, you should have another."

She'd been raised by a bone-skinny woman who espoused never eating a second serving of anything. Despite the doctrine being tattooed on Trish's brain, Tony Corcarelli was the kind of guy who could convince a girl to splurge. A classic bad boy, he was capable of more harm than good. But the good…*Mmm. Mmm. Mmm.*

Trish shook her head, scattering the thoughts that had her wallowing in adolescent purgatory, and reached for a more comfortable, competent topic. "How's the Jorgen's sofa coming along?"

"Should be done tomorrow. I can have the wingbacks ready next week." There wasn't a wrinkle on or around his lips, just smooth, perfectly puffed skin that circled a mouth decorated with teeth so white they were a sin on a man that dark.

"That's fine. I'm still waiting on the completion of a couple inlaid rugs, but the sooner the better. I want to keep this project on time." She sounded professional…and uptight, which was out of place for their surroundings but so much better than sounding like a crushing teen.

"So don't go changing the fabric on me again." He dropped his chin to his chest and regarded her through wide, smoky eyes. "Ya hear?" And then he winked.

Her stomach tumbled, churning the cake she'd eaten into cream.

"There you are." Jackson wrapped a sweaty hand around her bicep. "I have to go."

Tony lifted his full brows. "Duty calls, Doc?"

"Something like that."

But Trish knew better. Jackson wasn't on-call. He simply wasn't fond of the Corcarellis, something she'd learned on the car ride to the restaurant when he called them "Jersey Shore without the booze." The comment nagged Trish until she couldn't dismiss it as a poor attempt at humor, so she added it to the mental column of negatives vs. positives she kept for all her dates.

"Enjoy the rest of your evening, kids," Tony said with another crooked grin and a bob of his brows as he maneuvered around them. It was the kind of look that insinuated the rest of Trish's evening would be filled with hot, sticky, adventurous sex.

Trish would be lucky if she got a goodnight kiss. Looking up at prune-faced Jackson, she sighed. Three dates in, and already the negatives assigned to his list dipped perilously close to the kiss-off line.

"Tony, wait." A frilly-dressed, raven-haired girl shoved between Trish and Jackson to scurry after Tony.

Trish watched Tony turn and catch his little cousin as she leapt into his arms. The heartfelt, unscripted gesture made her smile, but when she turned back to Jackson he was scowling.

"These people have no manners," he grumbled. "And too many kids."

Thirty minutes later, after enough goodbyes, *arrivedercis*, and double-cheek kisses, Trish tucked inside Jackson's Porsche and listened to his continued complaints.

"That was a waste of three hours."

"I disagree. Nonna turning eighty-five is a big deal."

He rolled his eyes. "She's not *your* grandmother. None of those people are related to you—thank God. You could've sent a card and some flowers. Why subject yourself to that circus?"

That circus was all Trish wanted from life—not that specific circus, but a circus of her own. Loud, brash, unconditional love, not the kind of love that was earned by good behavior and hefty bankrolls. She sighed, because this part of getting to know someone in order to ascertain compatibility was always the most uncomfortable. "I'm adopted."

"Oh." He glanced at her as he adjusted his grip on the steering wheel. "I didn't know that."

Considering how much Jackson adored her surgeon father and socialite mother, she couldn't help but wonder if he was disappointed she didn't share the sacred DeVign genes.

"It's not really a big deal until I'm around a family like the Corcarellis," Trish continued. "Then I start to wonder what my biological family is like."

Road noise swirled between them as she waited patiently for his reaction.

He snorted. "If you ask me, that's dangerous thinking. I mean obviously you're better off now. Look how lucky you are. Hell, I'd stand in line to be adopted by the DeVigns."

She bet he would. "Yes, well, there's something to be said for knowing where you came from. Don't you think?"

"If I came from a family like the Corcarellis, I'd never want to know. Somebody needs to gift them with a lifetime supply of birth control so they stop polluting the gene pool." He laughed.

She clenched her hands in her lap and stared out the window at the shadowy shapes and lighted signs flying by. "I'll skip the nightcap, Jackson. Just drop me off at home."

"Oh. Hey." He slowed at a stoplight and stretched an arm across the top of her headrest. "I was kidding. I mean, they're accommodating enough. They're just rough around the edges, and it takes some getting used to." He smiled as he leaned closer, and for a second, hope bubbled in Trish's chest. "For a guy like me who'd rather have non-anesthetized surgery than kids, it's a real stretch to relate."

Every one of those stupid, hope-filled bubbles popped. "The light is green," she said, redirecting his attention to the road and her attention to the nauseous pit in her stomach.

She was tired of this; tired of getting her hopes up only to have them trashed. At thirty-two, according to her calculations, eight good baby-making years remained. She'd spent the last two years methodically dating, hoping for a ring and white dress. But when she imagined a lifetime with each prospect, and concluded it was more like a life sentence, she lowered her standards. After all, she was an independent woman who didn't need a man to help her raise a child. But she did need a man to help her make one…and for more than his sperm. She wanted his family history, too. The impersonal, anonymity of creating a baby with a bodiless stranger from a donor clinic wouldn't work. She wanted her baby to have a complete medical history, intergenerational stories, and at least a quarterly look at his or her dad.

"Are you sure you don't want that nightcap?" He parked in front of her house and flashed a suggestive grin.

"I'm sure." She'd rather have a baby. "My stomach isn't feeling right."

"Maybe it was the cake," he said as she opened the car door. "Who likes anise birthday cake anyway?"

She stood up and spun around. "I like anise birthday cake." And with that, she slammed the car door on his bewildered face.

"I'll call you tomorrow," he sputtered out his open window as she clip-clopped around the front of the car to her stone walk.

Don't bother, she thought.

Talk about a disappointing night. She should've had a second piece of cake.

• • •

Tony pulled the burlap tight around the wingchair's retied springs and fired staples from his gun into the wooden frame. He could tell a lot about a person by the condition of their furniture. This particular piece belonged to a newly minted chief of radiology and his wife, a friend of Trish. Before Tony could repair the split and crumbling frame, he'd had to remove three layers of dollar-table, outdated fabric, foul-smelling Dacron, and way too much foam rubber. The haphazard upholsteries told a rags-to-riches tale. When Tony was done, these once sad and neglected chairs would flank the finest fireplace in a Trish DeVign-decorated home. Something that didn't come cheap.

"Why don't you ever answer your freaking phone? Ma's been trying to get ahold of us all day." Angie barged into the garage like she owned the place…Well, technically she did. It was attached to her house, but Tony paid rent to use the space as his sometimes-upholstery shop. He couldn't very well upholster sofa-sized items in his downtown efficiency.

He kept his eyes on the staple line. "What's wrong with your phone?"

"My phone? I was onsite all day. You expect me to hear a phone ringing over a floor sander? You weren't here, were you? You were out on your bike."

"Maybe. What's it matter to you?"

"It matters, Tony. It matters."

That's what the women in his life—and there were a lot of them—were always telling him. Nonna, Ma, Angie, and his aunts were forever pressing him to sell the bike, cover the tattoos, and quit playing with furniture so he could take his place at the helm of Pop's carpentry company.

No, thank you.

Becoming a carpenter and taking over the business hadn't done Angie any good. The responsibility robbed her of free time and fun. Besides, Tony already owned his own business, contracting out his upholstery services. The business was small and nondescript, which left his freedom intact.

"What'd Ma want?" he asked, rather than stoke his sister's perennially pissy mood by defending his life's direction.

"I don't know. I can't reach her now. The line's busy. How hard is it to get call waiting and caller ID?"

For a woman who still couldn't figure out the TV remote? Hard.

Strains of "Born to Be Wild" echoed above the air compressor.

"That's her," Angie yelled, pointing in the direction of his phone.

"You answer it," Tony said, preferring to spare himself the gory details of which cousin said what, more than a week ago at Nonna's birthday party, and why aunts X, Y, and Z were no longer speaking.

Angie kicked his thigh with her steel-toed boot as she walked by on her way to answer his phone. "Why is nothing ever important to you?"

As he listened to his sister answer their mother's call, he winced at his stinging thigh and traded the staple gun for an old-fashioned hammer and tacks. Wailing on the metal wedges would help. He had news for his too-serious-for-her-own-good sister, lots of things were important to him. Fun topped the list, with happiness running a close second, followed by friends who fed the fun and happiness.

"Oh God, no," Angie sobbed, and then wailed. "Tony, Nonna has ovarian cancer."

The mallet slipped from his hand.

As much as they drove him crazy, family was important, too.

An hour later, Tony was packed like a sardine into Nonna's galley kitchen with a collection of aunts and uncles who watched the stricken woman stir sauce despite the horrible news.

"I give it to God," she announced, raising one palm to the ceiling. "I no take it back."

There were a few amens, but as Tony looked around the room, he was struck by the paleness of the usually olive faces. And there were tears, but only when Nonna wasn't looking. And there were whispers of sentences he couldn't quite catch.

Stage IV. Too late for surgery. Chemo. Radiation. Prayers.

He felt sick, like he swallowed a jar of lug nuts and couldn't cough them up, let alone crap them out. And when the bowls of food started around the table, he couldn't eat.

He pushed away his chair, knowing the bathroom was the only rational escape. If he left the house, someone was bound to snitch, and once again he'd be a disappointment; the Corcarelli son not man enough to face the truth. Away from the heavy emotions, he flipped the lid down on the toilet and pulled his cell phone from his pocket. Rather than dwell on the turmoil twisting his guts in knots, he'd dwell on his fantasy football team's lousy performance. His wide receivers tanked, and there were never any good ones available after the draft.

Tap. Tap. Tap.

Tony looked at the door. "Occupied." And yet he couldn't stay much longer, knowing someone waited, unless he wanted to look like an inconsiderate pig. So he hurried up and dropped a running back, picked up a defense, and took a deep breath before he opened the bathroom door.

Nonna stood on the other side. "Antonio." She smooshed his cheeks in her scratchy, onion-scented hands and smiled the saddest smile he'd ever seen.

All he could do was hug her, squish her weathered body against him and wish he were strong enough to expunge the cancer with one good squeeze. "Love you, Nonna."

She pushed out of the hug and patted his cheek. "Why you want to be alone?"

Of all things…she was bringing up his marital status today. "I'm not alone, Nonna. I have all of you."

Both of her hands patted his face. "Life should be shared."

"And I *am* sharing my life." He slid his hands around her wrists and held them in his.

"No wife. No *bebe*." She nodded. "You make a good priest."

He bit back a laugh. A tattooed, Harley-riding priest. Come to think of it, he'd like to see that. But not him. No way. He was pretty sure celibacy was bad for his health.

"I'm fine, Nonna."

But she wasn't.

She nodded and shuffled past him to the bathroom. He wondered if she was going in to get away—like him. But if losing Pops taught him anything, it was that cancer left nowhere to hide.

"Tony, you need to be out here for this." Ma poked her head into the hallway and flagged him back into the dining room.

Aunt Josie was speed talking in a whisper when he walked into the room. "How do you know she can fly?"

"I'll check with the doctor," Aunt Carmella said.

"I think it's a wonderful idea," Ma added.

"Aunt Carmella and Uncle Gene have offered to take Nonna back to Lucca for a couple weeks," Angie explained in Tony's ear. "And when she gets back from Italy, Aunt Jo and Uncle Mike are going to surprise her by flying her brother in from California. Sort of like a surprise bucket list."

Tony nodded. A lot could happen during ten minutes holed up in a bathroom.

"I'm going to become Catholic," Ma announced. Her sisters-in-law gasped.

Angie flashed a look at Tony. Even Dad's illness hadn't prompted a gesture like that. But in the years after his death, Ma and Nonna had grown close, close enough that Ma declared her the mother she'd never had. And now this? Talk about grand gestures.

Tony watched as Angie wrapped her arms around their mother's neck and squeezed. "I want to do something, too," Angie said. "I'll have to think about it though. Tony, what about you?"

If the burn from the air hitting his wide eyes was any indication, he looked like a deer in headlights. His family stared back at him.

"Take your time, Tony. Something will come to you."

But all around him, they didn't look convinced.

Nonna shuffled into the kitchen. "*Mangia. Mangia.*" She pointed at the table full of food.

With the conversation stalled, everyone took their seats and ate—everyone except for Tony. He stared at his pasta, in between glances at Nonna. His family was united in giving her months—hopefully years—to remember. They expected him to join in. He'd ignored their expectations without a care before, but this time was different.

Something will come to you.

Nonna slurped a noodle into her mouth and offered him a small smile. She wanted him to join the priesthood or fall in love.

Anyway Tony looked at it, he was screwed.

CHAPTER TWO

Trish squeezed a Murano vase between her forearm and bicep while she carried a trash bag stuffed with throw pillows. Using her free hand, she punched a code into the lock box hanging from the Jorgen's front door, and removed the key to the monstrous French provincial home. Once inside, she dropped the bag of pillows on the Carrera marble floor and admired the glossy white woodwork and matte gray walls. The design was crisp, clean, and sterile, which was exactly what Johann wanted. However, the colorful vase in the crook of her arm and the whimsical chandelier hovering above the entryway were bright, fun, and creative, which was exactly what Amanda wanted. To an interior designer, few things were as satisfying as fusing opposite tastes into one harmonious space.

Kicking her heels aside, Trish walked barefoot over the ice-cold tile. The Jorgens had asked for a runner, but she talked them into leaving the gleaming tile bare. After all, children racing down the stairs and weaving into the living room and out through the dining room could trip on a rug's edges. Not to mention how much easier it would be to power a riding toy along a smooth, stone surface. She smiled, because even better than fusing opposites was creating a beautiful home that wouldn't crumble under the blessed bedlam of babies.

Setting the vase on a Grecian-style sofa table and family heirloom the couple received as a wedding present, Trish admired the living room, which was anchored by a Chippendale sofa that had been expertly reupholstered by Tony. She ran her fingertips over the black-and-silver jacquard print and visualized the complementing wingchairs. She'd done good. She always did good when it came to decorating houses. If the rest of her life could be so simple…

Trish wandered to the high-gloss white bookshelves that sandwiched floor-to-ceiling windows, and adjusted Johann and Amanda's family photos. She tried to concentrate on the gilded frames instead of the sentimental scenes, but Amanda's pregnancy portrait caught her eye. Ethereal and joyful, the black-and-white photo made Trish's stomach cramp until, with a tiny growl, she banished the longing and turned her back on the photos. She marched through the living room and into the hallway, determined to reach the pillows and keep her mind focused on work. Self-pity was not acceptable while standing in a home she had decorated from million-dollar top to million-dollar bottom.

Two steps from the plastic bag, her phone vibrated against her hip. She freed the white rectangle from her tunic and grimaced at the caller ID. Her mother. And Trish knew exactly why she was calling.

"I haven't talked to Jackson," Trish said without offering a hello.

"Darling, what are you waiting for? I cannot bear for you to call Aunt Clarise and decline your 'plus one' simply because you've tossed another eligible man aside. How embarrassing. Call him. Beg him to escort you. It's the only way."

Trish turned her head to muffle a groan. "Begging a man to be my escort is embarrassing, too."

"Pick your poison, dear. It's either show up alone after RSVP'ing for two, or swallow your pride and grovel to Jackson. Who knows, you might have such a lovely evening he'll ask you out again. Wouldn't that be wonderful?"

"I don't want him to ask me out again. We weren't compatible."

"Nonsense. He's successful. You're successful. He's handsome. You're beautiful. Your father likes him. He likes your father. What more could you want?"

Trish's stomach cramped again. "Mother, I have to go. I'm at Amanda's house, waiting on a delivery, and then I have to be at Meyer's."

"Fine. But, darling, call him...before it's too late."

Silence echoed through the empty house as Trish stood frozen in the foyer. She didn't want to ask Jackson for anything, but she didn't want to show up to this wedding alone, opening herself up to questions about her relationship status and the pity that went along with being over thirty and single. What to do?

She walked then, returning the phone to her pocket. Maybe she would go alone. It wasn't like she deserved anyone's pity.

Her mother was right about one thing—Trish was successful. She was independent and thriving really. If it weren't for the popcorn popper of genetic unrest going off in her chest, life would be perfect. She snatched the bag of pillows and wondered again if she shouldn't try to find her biological parents in hopes of calming her restlessness.

A rumble followed by two clangs attracted her attention, and Trish pushed aside sheer curtains for a look outside before opening the front door. A white delivery truck emblazoned with the turquoise-and-black emblem of Trish DeVign Interior Design backed into the governor's driveway, stopping several feet from the front of her car. She stepped onto the stoop as Angie hopped down from the passenger seat.

"Delivery," Angie said, stomping her jeans down her legs and then adjusting the cuffs over the tops of her work boots.

Trish appreciated the juxtaposition of traits that made up her best friend. There wasn't a man in the business as skilled with a circular saw and wood as Angie Corcarelli, but when the girl shed the jeans and boots and slipped into something sleek, she was a knockout. The problem was Angie would just as soon *knock out* a suitor than flirt with him.

"Hey there," Trish called, stifling a laugh.

"Hey. You look happy despite two huge project deadlines. What gives? Wait. Don't tell me you're going out with Jackson again." Angie wrinkled her nose and shook her head. "Seriously. Don't tell me that. He was a stiff."

"I'm not going out with Jackson again."

"Are you telling me that 'cause I told you to tell me that or are you serious?" She ripped a rubber band off her wrist and stretched her arms behind her head to make a ponytail out of her ebony hair.

"I'm serious." Trish heard the cargo door roll up, and she walked toward the back of the truck, eager for a glimpse at the goods.

"Then why were you smiling?"

"No real reason. I'd been talking to my mother, which so did not make me smile and…"

Tony jumped off the tailgate.

Gone was the $800 suit, and in its place was his "uniform" of black T-shirt and threadbare jeans, both of which clung to his well-sculptured body like frosting to cake. *Yum.*

"Hey, Boss Lady. I got something for ya." He grinned. "Where do ya want it?"

A million indecent answers jockeyed for space in Trish's head.

"Where do you think she wants two wingchairs, jackass?" Angie jumped onto the tailgate and released the ramp lock. "Move so we can get this done. I have better things to do than play delivery girl."

Tony shook his head. "You're lucky years of abuse from you Corcarelli women have worn me down. I take orders so well I don't even argue." Rather than walk up the ramp, he pressed his palms to the tailgate and with a flex of his glorious forearms and biceps, lifted himself into the truck.

Trish held in a whimper and distracted herself with Angie and Tony's bickering. She'd known them long enough to know it was all in fun. Sure, they grated on each other's nerves, but when it came down to it, they loved each other, because they were made of the same parts. She suspected love like that felt different than any love she'd ever known.

"Watch your step, Ange. Slow and easy," Tony called.

As they maneuvered down the ramp, Trish tried to focus on the black plastic covering the furniture, hoping for a peek at what was underneath. But as Tony passed, she noticed what was underneath his shirt sleeve instead.

Tattooed Italian words circled his lean, chiseled bicep. Each letter rode the swell of muscles as he hoisted the chair. She wondered what the words meant, and she stared harder, trying to pronounce them in her head, only to find herself wondering what it would feel like to have those muscles contracting beneath her hand.

"The door," Angie yelled.

Crap. "Yep." Trish scrambled ahead of them to open the front door.

Angie brushed by first. Then Tony, and as he did, he looked at Trish and smiled. "You're gonna like what you see."

Trish watched him walk down the hall, his blue jeans slinging low across his hips. Yeah, she liked what she saw—a lot more than she should. Talk about a waste of time. The man was nowhere near father material. If she wanted to have fun and forget about her little lists and ticking biological clock, then Tony was her man, but...

"Are you waiting for a big reveal?" Angie called from the other room. "Get in here."

Trish blinked, realizing she was still standing in the foyer, door open wide along with her mouth. "I'm coming," she said, rushing down the hall, shaking her head.

She'd always been hyper-focused on her goals and single-minded when it came to achieving them, but this recent uptick in time spent dwelling on children was taking its toll. She didn't need to be worried about babies and baby daddies. She needed to be worried about finishing the Jorgen's home before they returned from Sweden, and finding a replacement date for her cousin's wedding. She could be happy without a baby. She *was* happy without a baby.

Get a grip, she thought as she turned the corner and walked into the living room. But any chance of that evaporated when she saw Tony sitting cross-legged in the wingchair.

"So?" He grinned, propping his elbows on the shimmering, striped fabric, showing off the large star and vines tattooed on the underside of his forearm. "You like?"

God, she smiled, because there was something about the man that made her giddy. Aside from the beautiful face and delicious body, there was this aura that drew her in and wrapped her up in a blanket of happiness she wished she could take with her wherever she went.

The chair was nice, too.

"Hurry up. Let's get the other one." Angie clomped out of the room.

Tony stood, still smiling, and turned to the chair. "Personally, I think it's some of my best work."

"Me too." Trish stood beside him, breathing in warm air with a hint of woodsy cologne. She imagined sweat from the labor diluted the scent, and she wondered what he smelled like the night of Nonna's party, when he was impeccably dressed. She snapped her head to look at him, imagining him in that suit again. "Would you…?" But her mouth slammed shut before the rest of the stupid idea escaped.

"Would I what?" One eyebrow raised in her direction.

Now she'd done it. The scattered matter she called a brain had finally made a fatal mistake. Taking Tony Corcarelli—no matter how good he looked in a suit—to her cousin's wedding was not a practical idea. And yet, as he stood there, smiling down at her with a gleam of mischief in his eye, she couldn't help but think he was just what she needed, a break from this exhausting pursuit of pregnancy. She deserved that once in a while. Didn't she?

"Holy hell!" Angie's voice echoed through the house. "A little help out here."

Trish shook away the heady thoughts and turned, walking toward the door. "Never mind, let's help her before she blows. I can't have her blowing. We have twenty eight-panel doors to hang over at Meyer's."

• • •

Tony followed Trish into the hallway, watching her dirty blonde hair swoosh between her shoulder blades. The minute his brain registered the dirty in blonde, his gaze dropped to her ass, swinging against the fabric of her mid-thigh sweater. Her uptight posture and coordinated clothing made him smile, because over the last two years he'd learned he had a knack for flustering her. If she were anyone other than his sister's best friend and the woman who contracted his upholstery work, he'd have flustered her good and hard a long time ago.

"Tony, you're screwing with my schedule." Angie stood on the tailgate, one hand on her hip, the other hand wrapped around her phone. "And now you're going to have to wait fifty-three seconds."

"For what?"

"Sh." Angie raised the phone to her face. "No way. Mother f…" Her fingers flew across the screen. "Come on. Come on. Come on." She tapped her foot so hard against the bottom of the truck, the metal rattled. "Nope." Her fingers raced again. "Ha! Yes. Yes. Yes! Ten, nine, eight. Crap." Again with the typing until finally, with a fist pump, she leaped off the tailgate and landed in the driveway. "I won!"

"What?" Trish asked.

"You're looking at the proud owner of a 1948 Cadillac convertible."

"Sweet." If there was one thing Tony and Angie agreed upon, it was the value of a sick set of wheels.

"I'm glad you think so, because you're going to need to help with the upholstery. This one is red and according to the picture Mom gave me, we need white." She walked back up the ramp and into the truck.

Tony followed. "Why do *we* need white? It's your car."

Angie bent over at the waist and hooked her hand beneath the chair. "Let's go. Lift. Nonna and Nonno had their first date in a black Caddy convertible, but with white upholstery. This is my contribution to her wish list."

Damn. Tony lifted the chair into his arms and walked backward down the ramp, all the while thinking he was once again the slacker of the bunch. "I can help with the seats."

"Good." Angie smiled. "She's going to flip."

"I can't believe you guys are doing this. How cool." Trish held open the front door.

Tony tossed her a *thank you* with a nod of his head. The wish list was cool, and he wanted to be a part of the coolness, but how cool was it if his only contribution was being the upholstery boy to Angie's big idea?

Nobody appreciated the upholstery boy.

"Tony, this stuff is unbelievable. You are a rock star." Trish was standing next to the first wingchair, having bypassed Tony and Angie to enter the living room through the dining room instead of the hall. She stood there beaming at the chair, and then at him like he'd hung the moon.

Okay, so nobody appreciated the upholstery boy except Trish DeVign. He could do a lot worse. Still, that wasn't going to impress Nonna.

"Done." Angie swiped her hands as she walked toward the hall. "I'll be in the truck, Tone. Give me a few minutes so I can call this guy about paying for the car and getting it delivered."

"Thank you," Trish called. "I'll see you at Meyer's."

Tony turned back to the chairs and Trish, who had removed the plastic covering and settled onto the cushion, crossing her long legs and bouncing one barefoot with red-painted toes in his direction. As she sat, she rubbed her palms over the arms of the chair and breathed deeply enough that he risked hypnosis by the rise and fall of her breasts. Not the sort of thing he wanted to notice about a woman he couldn't pursue.

"You really do great work."

He smiled and stepped closer, because he was a gentleman who'd just been complimented. "Thank you." He squatted and ran his hand along the nailhead trim, grazing her covered calf muscle, because he was a guy who liked the way her face flushed whenever he stood too close. "I'm glad you like it. When you're in need of my skills again, you know where to find me." And then he stood, taking two steps back toward the hall, because even a screw-up like him knew where to draw the line.

She sat ramrod straight, gripping the arms of the chair. "Tony, I need a favor."

He stopped. "What's up?"

"I need a...guest for my cousin's wedding on Saturday. Would you happen to be interested?"

"I take it the good doctor wasn't so good."

A nervous chuckle escaped her lips. "Not good at all. And I RSVP'd for two with the hope that he'd still be around, and now my mother is driving me crazy, saying I can't embarrass myself and her by cancelling this late in the game. I'm stuck."

It was Tony's turn to chuckle. "So you want me to unstick you?"

She shrugged, managing cute, coy, and sexy with one pouty-mouthed look. "Would you?"

If he was sane and sensible, no, he wouldn't. "Absolutely. What time should I pick you up?"

"Thank you," she breathed on a noisy exhale. "We should leave at three, but I'll drive."

"You don't trust my driving?"

"It's a wedding, Tony, and I'm wearing a dress. You should wear a suit, like the one you wore to Nonna's party." He liked the way she pulled her bottom lip between her teeth when she paused for a breath. "Dress clothes can't be worn on the back of a motorcycle."

An image of her creamy leg stretching out from beneath a short skirt and hanging alongside the chrome of his bike made his skin itch. He grinned to cover the not-so-innocent thought. "No bike. Got it. I'll pick you up at three." And before she could protest, he turned around and walked away.

He'd never been the kind of guy to let a woman down, and that was a blessing and curse. Now he needed a car worthy of escorting Trish DeVign to a family wedding, in addition to a grand gesture for Nonna's wish list.

Talk about pressure.

CHAPTER THREE

Tony parked his bike in a spot marked *Reserved for Joyce Richards*. Of course he wasn't Joyce Richards, but he knew his cousin's executive assistant wouldn't need the spot until she returned from vacation. Hitching his right leg behind him, he swung his boot over the seat and nodded at a well-dressed businessman who eyed him suspiciously. No doubt the stuffed suit thought Tony was associated with one of Vin's criminal clients.

Just for fun, Tony picked up his pace, riding the guy all the way to the elevators, and then, at the last possible second, Tony darted right and took the stairs. He was still chuckling when he pushed against the plaque that read *Vincent Spada Law Offices, State and Federal Criminal Defense*.

One foot inside the cushy office and the receptionist's blue eyes peered over a high-back desk. "Hiya, Tony."

He propped elbows on the shiny wood and smiled. "Hey, Mavis. You're looking beautiful today."

She rolled back her chair and smoothed a palm over her giant ball of a belly. "I feel like a beached whale. Swear to God."

"It'll be worth it."

"How would you know?"

"Big family, remember? And that's what all my aunts say."

She grimaced. "I hope so." And then with a sigh, she pointed over her head to the hallway behind her. "Vinnie's in the boardroom alone. Go ahead and go back, but be careful. He's in a mood."

Which could only mean one thing. Vin lost a case, and Vin, a former marine, hated to lose.

The boardroom door was opened a crack, so Tony nudged it wider to see Vin holding a flimsy-looking putter between two gorilla-like hands and aiming for a tipped-over plastic cup.

"You lose one?" Tony asked as he entered the room and closed the door behind him.

"Yep." Vin dropped the putter and kicked the golf ball, which missed the cup and collided with the baseboard on the far side of the room. "I hate to lose."

"It happens to the best of us."

"Right. I suppose you understand what it feels like to watch a man be locked away for a crime he didn't commit. It's probably like screwing up the vinyl on a kitchen chair." He slapped a palm to his forehead and groaned. "I'm sorry. That was lousy. Even for me."

"Don't worry about it. You're upset." The words stung, but they gave Tony something to use as leverage.

Vin grabbed his suit coat off the back of a chair before he sat, taking a few audible inhales and exhales, like he was trying to clear his mind. "So what's up? Any changes with Nonna?"

Tony sat, too. "Nope. Not that I know of. I saw Angie an hour ago and she didn't say anything."

"Good."

"Yep."

Vin whipped out his phone and tapped his fingers on the screen. "I tracked down those Italian tenors she loves through a colleague, and I'm trying to book a private performance."

Damn. More wish list talk. The family was determined to send Nonna out in style. Tony nodded at Vin, despite the knot in his gut.

"Have you figured out what you're going to do?"

"Working on it," Tony said, avoiding eye contact so as not to see the telltale stare. Vin, more than anyone else in the family, wanted to see Tony get his act together. A marine wasn't happy until the rest of the world towed the line.

"Why don't ya put some of that money to good use and buy her a newly discovered solar system. Name it Corcarelli? Ya know? Preserve the last name for posterity."

Tony glanced at Vin who leaned back in his chair, staring at the overhead florescent lights, resting huge hands across his belly. By the blank expression on his face, Tony knew he was serious.

It wasn't the first time someone rode him about his familial duty to have a son and preserve the Corcarelli name. Tony's father had been the only Corcarelli male, and it seemed legendary that he fathered the only son. Every once in a while, someone reminded Tony that if he didn't have a son too, he'd take the Corcarelli name to the grave. Nice thought, huh? But a star seemed corny, not to mention insulting. He couldn't imagine Nonna calling it an even trade.

"Thanks for the idea, but I have a few of my own," Tony lied. "You'll be the first to know when I decide which one to go with."

Vin sniffed loudly, calling bull on Tony's diversion tactic.

"Hey, can I borrow the Ferrari?" Tony knew the question would eradicate the topic of Nonna's wish list.

"What?" Vin straightened and propped an elbow on the table. His huge silver watch glistened. "Are you kidding me? It's a classic. I don't even let *me* drive the Ferrari...much."

"It's one night, Vin. One night. I won't drink a drop of alcohol. I'll keep it to the side roads and under thirty. I'll...Name it. Whatever you want me to do, I'll do. I just need that car."

"What's her name?"

"Trish DeVign."

"Jesus, Mary, and Joseph, you've lost your mind," Vin said, slapping a palm to the table. "She's your bread and butter, man. Why would you mess it up by dating her?"

"It's not a date. She needs an escort to a family wedding."

Vin raised one bold, black brow and zeroed in on Tony's left arm tattoos. "And she asked *you?*"

Tony smiled. "She likes how I look in a suit. And if she likes how I look in a suit, she's going to love how I look in a suit in your car."

"Take my Lexus."

"That's pathetic. That's an old man's fat ride, and I won't subject my image to that."

Vin whipped a pencil in Tony's direction.

Tony ducked. "Hey, you owe me."

"For what?"

"You said I screwed up a vinyl kitchen chair. I'll have you know I don't screw up, and I don't use vinyl. Nasty, cheap stuff."

Vin roughed his face in his hands, releasing a low growl that had Tony on the edge of his seat. "Fine. You can borrow it, but only because I was an ass earlier, and I don't want you to look like an ass at this wedding."

Tony jumped to his feet and kissed Vin on the back of the head. "I'll do you proud, man."

"Just bring her home in one piece."

"Oh, eh, I have no intentions of bringing Trish DeVign home." Because once he got her there, he didn't trust himself to behave.

Vin scowled. "The car. Bring the car home in one piece."

Now *that* Tony could do.

• • •

Trish stood in the Meyer's laundry room doorway, looking out over the four-car garage turned Angie's temporary workshop. She watched as Angie clamped a hinge jig to a door and reached for the wood router. The minute Angie flipped the switch, saw noise would drown out any words Trish wanted to say…and that was the problem. What words did Trish want to say? She warred with herself, hoping Angie would flip the switch and make it impossible to speak.

Hunched over the door, router in hand, Angie glanced at Trish through clear safety goggles. "Do you need something?"

Trish flinched. She'd been putting this off for hours now, and she wasn't sure why. Taking Tony to her cousin's wedding wasn't a big deal. Was it? If it wasn't, then why did her stomach feel as if she ordered fifty bolts of non-returnable fabric in the wrong color every time she thought about telling Angie?

"How much longer for the doors?" Trish asked, stalling.

Angie straightened. "What's wrong?"

"Nothing."

"Don't tell me nothing. You never question my work unless you're stressing about something. What's wrong?"

Trish stepped into the sawdust-scented garage, skirting a pile of two-by-fours that stretched across sawhorses. She stopped on the other side of the six-panel door Angie had propped against her worktable. "Nothing's wrong. The doors look great. The bedroom built-ins are beautiful. The window seat is breathtaking. Your guys are ahead of schedule with the deck. And…I asked Tony to escort me to my cousin's wedding."

Angie adjusted her safety goggles and laughed, but as her laughter died, her eyes widened. She set the router aside. "Oh God, you're serious. Why? Why would you want to do that?"

"I don't have a choice. I mean, I do. I could ask a stranger or an ex-boyfriend, neither of which is appealing, or I could go alone, but can you imagine my mother's horror over her daughter doing something socially unacceptable like attending a wedding alone?"

"Yes, but I can also imagine your mother's horror over her daughter doing something socially unacceptable like having Tony Corcarelli as her date. I'd go with a stranger."

"It's not a date. It's a favor."

"It's a disaster waiting to happen. And you know it, that's why you didn't want to tell me."

Trish stared at the white embroidered letters of *Corcarelli Carpentry Co.,* which were stitched into the red fabric covering

Angie's heart. "I didn't want to tell you because I knew you'd object. You never give Tony enough credit. He's a good guy."

"You're blinded by his beauty like all unrelated, underused vaginas."

The distinctive sound of a male clearing his voice punctuated Angie's sentence. "I'm ready for another batch, Ange."

Angie gestured to three doors leaning against a far wall. "Take those. They're done. And for cripes sake, don't go banging up the woodwork."

Nino lowered his eyes, but nodded at his cousin as he lifted a door.

Trish choked down embarrassment as she watched him leave the garage, and then when she was sure he'd ventured out of earshot, she turned on Angie. "My vagina…" she whispered, fearing another crewmember would overhear the conversation, "is not underused."

Angie ripped the safety goggles off her face and leveled Trish with shiny brown eyes. "I'm talking about man-made orgasms, not man-made devices."

"Hush," Trish warned, but a giggle slipped out of her poorly pursed lips.

"Just remember, Tony's beauty comes with a price. This is a guy who drove a motorcycle six hours to Philly in the middle of the night because he was jonesing for cheesesteak. He slept on a park bench for two measly hours and then drove six hours home. You're going to get sucked into that happy-go-lucky vortex, and then he's going to let you down. As much as I love him, he sucks at being responsible and serious."

"He's never missed a deadline for me."

"Because he knows I would throttle him."

Trish smiled, because she knew Angie would, too. Still, she didn't think Angie's iron fist was the sole thing keeping a free-spirited man like Tony in line. He might be reckless, but he wasn't self-destructive like Angie made him out to be. "You're too hard on men."

Angie pushed the goggles onto her face. "Because not one of them is as good of a man as my dad was. You find me one that is, and then we'll talk."

That was a tall order. Trish hadn't known the man, but she knew the legend. Pasquale Corcarelli was one part mythical beast, the other part saint. He once rebuilt a house that had been obliterated by fire in time for the owners to host the Feast of the Seven Fishes despite three feet of snow and a flu-ravaged crew.

"Fair enough," Trish said, because one of these days, she was going to find that man for Angie. But first, she had to navigate her own wish list, something she intended to put on hold for one weekend. "You have nothing to worry about when it comes to me taking Tony to this wedding. I just want to have some fun."

Angie narrowed her eyes. "I don't want to think about you and my brother having fun. That's plain wrong."

"Because you're thinking of the wrong kind of fun." And now Trish was too. Sexy, sweaty, sticky fun that made her squirm. *That* was the wrong kind of fun, wasn't it? After all, the idea of Trish and Tony indulging in anything more sinful than two servings of wedding cake was absurd. They were about as compatible as olive oil and mineral water.

"Remember you said all of this when he turns on the charm."

Trish waved off Angie's skeptical gaze. She'd been subjected to Tony Corcarelli's good looks and crooked smiles for a couple years now. Surely she'd been exposed to the full extent of his harmless flirtations. For crying out loud, she'd seen him carry a sticky-fingered preschooler while he wore a designer suit. What could be more charming than that?

She pressed a palm to her stomach, staving off the psychosomatic cramps. "I'll be fine, Ange. You have nothing to worry about."

And Trish wasn't going to worry, either. For the first time in a long time, she was going to shed serious, wiggle out of worry, and focus on fun.

It was one night. How much trouble could she possibly get into?

CHAPTER FOUR

Tony owned two suits, one for weddings and one for funerals. Once, he mixed the pants from one suit with the jacket of the other, because the occasion was both a reason to celebrate and a reason to mourn. Back then, Tony knew Vin's marriage was destined for divorce before a single "I do." Some guys weren't meant to be married. Guys like Tony and Vin fit that bill.

Tucking the tails of his navy dress shirt into his black pants, Tony didn't think twice about wearing the same suit he'd worn to Nonna's party to the DeVign wedding. He looked damn good in the designer duds. Plus, he was getting his money's worth, something bound to make his more responsible family members proud.

With a paisley tie around his neck and a matching square of cloth in his lapel pocket, he double-checked his appearance in the mirror on the back of his bedroom door.

"I'd do me," he said with a smile, followed by a frown, because he didn't need to be thinking about getting laid when his date was Trish DeVign.

Grabbing his wallet and Vin's keys from the dresser, Tony headed out the door. The vintage Ferrari parked in the spot where his bike usually was startled him. For one, he loved his bike—missed her, even—and two, he couldn't believe Vin agreed to let him borrow the car. That was a true sign of familial love and respect.

Tony slipped the key into the lock, releasing the door, and slid inside. Gripping the leather steering wheel, he inhaled and exhaled, reminding himself of all the ways Vin could cause him pain and suffering should Tony put one mark on this car. But the sobering moment passed when Tony glanced into the rearview mirror, catching sight of his sleek hair and dark eyes. In this suit, in this car, nobody would suspect he was the upholstery boy. No way. He was a regular man of mystery.

"Bond, James Bond." He laughed as he fired up the engine.

Fifteen minutes later, he pulled alongside the curb of Trish's Shadyside home. Looking up at the lighted window of the fat dormer at the top of the historic foursquare, he wondered why one woman would tie herself to so much house. Maybe it was work-related, like a living, breathing interior design showroom, an idea that would've had merit if he didn't know Trish had an equally impressive office space around the corner on flashy Walnut Street. Being from a wealthy family was more than likely the culprit.

Out of the car, Tony locked the doors—like Vin demanded—even though he was only walking thirty feet to the porch. He knocked and then waited with his back to the door, his focus on the car's metallic paint, sparkling in the afternoon sun.

"Hey." The soft word sounded in unison with the click-clack of the opening door.

Tony turned and lost his breath, like the air around him created a vacuum, sucking every last drop from his chest. Trish wore a curve-hugging, grass-green dress that crisscrossed her breasts and showed off miles of creamy arm.

"Let me grab my purse," she said, offering a weak smile before she turned away from the door.

Two steps were all it took for him to notice the seam up the back of her black-print pantyhose, which were capped off with white-and-black retro pumps.

"Jesus, Mary, and Joseph," he breathed, hooking his finger inside his too-tight collar. "You look hot."

She glanced at him from her hunched over position in front of the foyer mirror, where she was pressing French-manicured fingertips to smooth a single strand of pearls. "Thank you." She gave a wobbly grin and looked back to her reflection in the mirror. "You sound surprised. I must look like hell every other day."

Had he really never complimented her before? If not, that was a travesty. In thirty-three years, he'd complimented hundreds of women for being a thousand times less attractive than Trish. It had to be the work thing. Maintaining professionalism under Angie's watchful eye must've rendered him speechless.

Then again, Trish had never worn fishnet stockings to work.

"You always look great," he said, hoping to make up for lost time. "It's just this outfit is over and above your usual work attire."

"Yeah, well it's hard to hang a cornice box in three-inch heels."

And that was a damn shame.

She dabbed at the corners of her glossy lips, and then turned to him. An inhale lifted her shoulders, and an exhale returned them to their regular place, a place that accentuated the shadowy, deep V between her breasts.

"Ready?" she asked.

No. Freaking. Way. He was dead. This was crazy.

She brushed by him without waiting for his answer, splashing his face with a gust of spicy air. Shit. Even her perfume smelled like a proposition.

"Wow." She stopped on the top step. "Now that's some car."

"And that's some dress," he said, getting a good look at the way the rayon cradled her curvy ass.

She glanced over her shoulder, eyes wide. "Tony, I'm having second thoughts about this."

At least now they were even.

• • •

Trish set a shaky hand on the railing and stared at the sex-on-wheels Tony called a car. It was safer than staring at him in that suit.

"I'm a good driver. I swear."

Nice to know, but she wasn't worried about his driving. She drew a shaky breath and held it until her lungs burned. "My family is very uptight," she rattled on an exhale. "They have expectations of me and my dates."

"And yet you wore those stockings."

"Tony." She spun around and leveled him with her most threatening look. "You have to behave."

He stepped closer and lowered his eyelids. "This is me behaving."

"I was afraid of that."

And then he grinned, and she really didn't care if he upheld one silly societal expectation. As long as he smiled like that, letting the dip in his cheek darken, he'd ease the minds of everyone in the room.

"Come on. We'll have fun." He bent his left arm in her direction.

She lifted her hand, but paused before she touched him, thinking about Angie's fear of Tony and Trish having the wrong kind of fun. But that was Angie's fear, not Trish's. She was a grown woman, capable of wrangling her wayward desires in favor of a pleasant, professional afternoon. Looping her arm through his, she tried not to care about the prickles on her skin as the heavy fabric of his suit coat brushed the underside of her upper arm.

"Don't make me regret this, Tony," she said as he led her down the porch steps.

When she looked at him, hoping to see his face sobered by her warning, he winked. "No worries, Boss Lady. I gotcha covered."

Which was an image she didn't need in her head, but an image that surfaced a few times—despite her best attempts at trampling it—on their way to the country club.

She kept the conversation work-related. He talked about the car. But in the silence lurked those stupid images, particularly one of Tony covering her while they had all sorts of the wrong kind of fun.

"So your people don't get married in a church?"

Her people. In an odd way she liked that he didn't call them her family, not that they weren't her family. They were the only family she'd ever known. But "her people" seemed to fit. She blinked a few times and faced him. "We're not particularly religious."

"A Corcarelli isn't married if he didn't get married in the church. If he wakes up the morning after a wedding on the beach or at the supper club, he's just broke as hell and living in sin."

She stared at him, watching his lips part into a grin. She couldn't imagine him conforming, following such a rule. Heck, she couldn't imagine him married. "So someday, will you get married in a church?"

He chuckled. "Marriage isn't really my thing. Too restrictive."

She had him pegged on that.

"But I'd like kids," he continued. "Kids are about the best part of life. Too bad they're kind of impossible without a wife, unless I want to risk custody battles with an ex-girlfriend who hoped to tie me down."

His words acted like a vise grip on Trish's lungs. She opened her mouth, but couldn't capture enough air to keep calm. She turned her head to hide her exaggerated breathing. And all the while her chest pushed against the bodice of her dress so hard she had to raise a hand to keep her breasts from popping out of the neckline.

"You okay?" he asked.

"Yeah, just hot." She pawed around the door for a handle to open the window.

When she looked at him, he was grinning. "I'm not going to tell you that opening a window won't help, because you'll still be hot. That wouldn't be me behaving. Right?"

She managed a small smile. "Right." And then she turned her attention out the open window, not caring one bit that the wind whipped the crud out of her French-twisted hair.

She had bigger worries.

Tony Corcarelli wasn't an option for her baby-making plans. He was Angie's brother. Trish squeezed her hands together hard enough to dig her fingernails into her skin. Angie would go ballistic if she knew Trish was thinking like this. Angie would remind Trish that Tony was a screw-up. He lived in a shoebox in a neighborhood famous for drunken bar fights. He drove a Harley, for cripes sake. His tattoos alone were enough to make Trish's mother faint. He'd never stepped foot on a college campus. He made up words like "whaddya" and "dontcha," and his family was the same—not that she didn't like his family. Trish loved his family, but the idea of her family, knowing his family was half of her child, well…

"Can I ask you something?"

"Sure," she choked out.

"Is there booze at this wedding? Not that I'm drinking anything but tonic water. You, on the other hand, look like you need a drink—or two. Relax," he said, giving her thigh a pat. "I'll take good care of you."

And he did.

"So what do you do for a living, Mr. Corcarelli?" Aunt Constance eyed him like he was more delectable than the wedding cake.

After being softened by his polished charms for four hours, Trish suspected he was.

"I own a furniture upholstery business." He grinned.

"Oh yes, I could tell you were a business owner. You have that air about you." She made an awkward sound, half giggle, half whimper.

Trish gripped the stem of her champagne glass and looked over her shoulder so she could cringe.

"It's a lovely wedding, and your daughter is a beautiful bride."

Again with the silly sound, but this time, instead of cringing, Trish smiled at her aunt. "Speaking of the bride, we should offer our congratulations while she's free. Excuse us, Aunt Constance."

Trish tugged on Tony's arm, but not before he took Aunt Constance's hand and smoothed it between his palms. "You take care."

The woman swayed a bit, prompting Tony to clutch her elbow and steady her.

"Ooh, my. Low blood sugar," she giggled. "Time to cut that cake." She waddled off with her head held high. It was a familiar scene.

Apparently Angie was right about unrelated vaginas and their reaction to Tony.

"What are you doing?" she asked, tugging Tony across the ballroom floor, not at all aware of where she was taking him.

"What do you mean what am I doing?"

"You're laying it on a little thick, don't you think?"

"You said behave."

"I did, but don't…" Trish attempted to swallow the unrest that had plagued her since their car ride, "try so hard."

How was she supposed to stop looking at Tony like a potential father for her baby if her family didn't stop fawning over him? It was the suit. She groaned into her champagne glass.

"Whaddya say?"

Whaddya. Exactly. "Nothing," she grumbled.

"Antonio, dear." Trish's mother excused herself from a small group and cornered Tony. "Would you suggest linen for an ottoman?"

"No, ma'am. I wouldn't. Linen may resist pilling and fading, but it soils and wrinkles." He leaned closer, as if he was going to whisper in her ear. "And that's not the kind of fabric you want handling feet."

"Just as I suspected." She grabbed hold of Tony's Trish-free arm and squeezed. "Thank you for taking my side on this. Oh, Rosemary." She let go and fluttered back to her group.

Trish frowned. "She could've asked me."

"I think she wanted to touch my bicep."

Like Trish was touching his bicep? Her palm flattened against his arm, while her fingers stretched to his triceps. A thick wool suit coat and broadcloth shirt weren't enough to mask the feel of his muscles, contracting beneath her hand.

She had to stop this slow slide out of sanity…fast.

"Let's dance." She let go of him, dropped her glass on a passing table, and powered through the crowd to the dance floor.

If she could keep him moving to this God-awful jazz music, she could get him sweaty enough to remove his coat and roll up his sleeves. One look at Tony's tattoos, and the DeVigns would be lining up to protect Trish from the hoodlum.

Not that he was a hoodlum, and not that she needed protection from him. It was more like she needed protection from herself.

When she reached the dance floor and turned around, she half expected Tony to have returned to their table. After all, she'd never known a guy who liked to dance outside of the requisite slow dance. Even now, the dance floor was filled with poky ladies and a couple half-soused old men.

But Tony was right behind her.

"Are you sure you can dance in that dress," he said, leaning his mouth so close to her ear his breath fluttered the curls at her temple.

"Stop it," she hissed, but there was little bite behind her words. The playful swat and nervous smile probably had something to do with that.

Shaking off the little thrill of having his lips so close to her face, Trish fisted her hands and lifted them to chest-height as she bounced on the balls of her feet. "Heavyweight linen would work fine for an ottoman used in a formal living room."

He stood there, not moving a muscle, not shedding a single bead of sweat. "Formal living rooms are a waste of space."

"Says the man who lives in a shoebox."

He shoved his hands into his pockets. "How would you know what I live in? You've never been to my place."

And she was going to keep it that way. "Dance. You look silly, standing there, watching me."

"I like watching you."

Zing! No little thrill that time. Her body nearly puddled at the truckload of heat he dumped over her. "Tony," she warned, but some errant impulse caused her to spin, showing off her grooving backside.

When she spun back around he was dancing, not the drunken flail of her sixty-something uncles, but a cocky toss of his head, and a smooth roll of his hips.

Who was sweating now? Beads tickled between her shoulder blades. Maybe her dancing was to blame. Although that would be pathetic—she hadn't been moving for more than five minutes.

He reached up and loosened his tie.

That-a-baby, she thought, remembering she was on a mission to prove that Tony Corcarelli was 100 percent wrong for her and her future plans.

But then he grabbed her hand, pulling her fast and hard against his chest.

"Hey," she protested, wiggling against his palm on the small of her back, but as she did, she realized her legs rested on either side of his thigh, and the fabric of her dress strained against his knee.

"What? You too old and stuffy for a good grind?" He gripped her right hand in his left hand as he lowered them both to the floor.

Her knees shook. Her heart raced. A steady stream of sweat spilled down her spine. She couldn't imagine how undignified this looked...which was exactly why she stayed. In his arms. With his body nearly infiltrating hers. If Tony wasn't going to shed the suit coat and brandish those tattoos, he could at least make a tawdry exhibition out of her, horrifying her family and dispatching them to her aid.

It was a plan she was certain would work, until the band lambasted her with a slow song, and Tony nuzzled his cheek to hers.

If the twinges in her stomach were any indication, this night was not going to end well.

CHAPTER FIVE

Tony didn't drink a drop of alcohol, so why was his head spinning? He stared at the beautiful woman sitting across the table from him. Tiny curls, wet from the sweat of their dancing, clung to the sides of her head. Her skin glowed a happy pink from the exertion. And he wondered—against his better judgment—if she looked like this after sex.

"Where are you kids headed after this?" Dr. DeVign swiped a white napkin across his mouth and then tossed it on the table.

"No place. This is it." Trish's eyes were wide as she nodded. "Such a great night. So tired. Big day tomorrow. Huge."

Tony hadn't just flustered her, he'd nearly incapacitated her. He knew it the moment she broke from his arms at the start of the slow dance only to come back here and take a seat in silence next to her mother.

"Very good. I have quite the day, too. Dolores, shall we give our best to the bride and groom, and be on our way?" Dr. DeVign didn't allow his wife to answer. He stood, lifted his jacket off the back of his chair and extended a hand to Tony. "It was nice meeting you, young man. Make sure Trisha gets home safely."

"Yes, sir," Tony said, standing to return the healthy grip.

Mrs. DeVign latched onto Tony's arm. "Don't rush out on our account. I'm sure you have time for one more dance." She looked at Trish, who was looking anything but eager to take her mother's advice. "Right, dear?"

"Leave the girl alone, Dolores." Walking behind Tony, Dr. DeVign took his wife's arm and led her from the table, pausing briefly to place a kiss on his daughter's forehead.

Tony watched the older couple fade into the thinning crowd, and then he slipped his hands into his pants pockets as he smiled at Trish. "How 'bout that dance?" he asked, even though he expected a refusal.

She shook her head. "I really am tired."

So was he....tired of skirting around the obvious attraction, but what was their alternative? Angie's steel-toed boot in his ass as she kicked him out of her garage, guaranteeing he'd lose his space to work—should Trish ever feel comfortable enough to hire him again.

He walked around the table and pulled back her chair, and when she stood, stopping inches from his chest, her face never lifting, he felt like a freaking martyr for putting the brakes on whatever was happening between them.

Tony hated brakes. He liked to go like hell, then back off the gas and coast until he came to a nice, easy stop.

"Thanks for coming with me tonight." Trish still wasn't looking at him. Instead, she pushed in her chair, fussed with a wedding favor, and smoothed the wrinkles from her dress. And then she walked to the door. Unlike her parents, she didn't exchange goodbyes with the bride and groom or a single relative, but she did nod sweetly at the wait staff, clearing plates from a table near the door.

She was a complicated creature. Tony was used to Ma and Angie, two women who put family above all others and told it like it was, whether he liked it or not. He was also used to overly eager twenty-somethings who clung to him at the bars, saying all sorts of things that made him blush. Him. Blush. Which wasn't easy.

It also wasn't easy to figure out where Trish DeVign fit in that mix.

She walked ahead of him, making a beeline for Vin's car. Normally, he'd ogle her ass and legs in the low streetlamp light, and imagine the shock on her face if he told her he wanted to see her in nothing but those heels. But tonight wasn't normal.

He stopped alongside Vin's $150,000 Ferrari.

See? Not normal.

After they settled into the car, Tony banished the uncomfortable silence with a twist of his wrist, firing the engine. The purring soothed his scattered thoughts, but didn't quiet them. For lots of reasons, he didn't want to screw up. Aside from avoiding Angie's temper and the loss of income, Tony liked Trish. He liked the way she didn't throw herself at him, and he liked the glimpse of playfulness beneath the professional exterior. In fact, he liked the combination so much he'd call her the marrying kind if a man was so inclined. Which he wasn't. And because he wasn't, anything beyond a goodnight kiss to Trish's cheek was out of the question.

The best thing he could do was get things back to normal.

"Are you mad at me because I said formal living rooms are a waste of space?" he teased.

She smiled, a smile that crinkled the skin around her eyes more than it curled her lips. "No. I'm not mad at you. I've just got a lot on my mind."

"Like decorating formal living rooms."

She chuckled, but she also gnawed the inside of her bottom lip. Being raised by a bunch of women made him an expert in female, nonverbal communication.

"If you want to talk, I'm good at listening," he said, gripping her headrest and twisting for a better view as he backed out of the parking spot. "Plus, I know what it's like to have a lot on my mind. Maybe I can help."

Her inhale and exhale echoed inside the car. "Tony, I'm sorry. I must seem silly, brooding about my little problems when your family is dealing with Nonna's illness."

"Problems are problems." He hugged the shoulder of the road, not wanting to take any chances with the oncoming traffic and Vin's car.

"Some problems are bigger than others. Angie said the cancer is inoperable."

These days everybody wanted to talk about Nonna. Her treatment. Her wish list. How much time she had left.

Tony hated funerals.

Sweaty hands gripped the steering wheel as he stared into oncoming headlights, trying not to relive every gory, emotional detail about his father's funeral, but the memories were strong enough to make him wince.

"I wish there was something I could do," Trish said, laying a hand on his thigh. His muscles contracted at the warmth of her palm.

He stared harder at the passing traffic. "Yeah, that seems to be the sentiment. "

"And that's the reason for the list."

"Yep. But that list's sort of become a thorn in my side."

"Why?"

"Because damned if I know what to do. I highly doubt a ride on a Harley's going to cut it, and I don't think she wants an upholstered rocking chair. She wants me to become a priest..." Trish laughed. "Exactly, or get married and have babies."

Trish stopped laughing on a tiny whoop. He looked at her, catching her eyes wide and her cheeks puffed, like she was holding her breath. "She's crazy, right?" he asked, waiting for Trish's lips to break open on a wave of fresh laughter.

But the laughter never came. Instead, she nodded and then turned her head so she faced the passenger window.

Maybe he disappointed her, too. He was getting good at that.

"I'm adopted," she said. "It's amazing for me to witness a real family coming together to lessen the pain of one of their own."

She tipped her head slightly, and he could've sworn he saw a glimmer of wet in the corner of her eye, alongside her nose.

He looked back to the road. "I didn't know you were adopted."

"Not many people do. I'm a little uncomfortable with the topic."

His chest puffed on the realization that she was telling him. "You shouldn't be uncomfortable. Family is more than blood, you know? I have a couple buddies who feel an awful lot like brothers to me. Just don't tell a Corcarelli I said that. They place an awful lot of credence on that 'blood-is-thicker-than-water' thing."

"I know they do. I watch you and Angie and it makes me sad I'll never know what that feels like."

"What? To want to punch the lights out of someone you love?" He chuckled. "Nah. She's a good kid. Tough on me, though. Woo wee. Tougher than Ma and Nonna. Those two sort of balance Angie out."

Tony had no idea what would happen once Nonna was gone.

More memories from the days following his father's funeral snuck into Tony's brain. *You gotta run the business, Tony. Dontcha wanna be like him?* Tony struggled for other memories, recent, stronger memories to push the bad ones away. The first one to come to mind was Trish on the dance floor.

He grabbed it in a sleeper hold. "Where'd you learn to dance like that?" he asked, not caring one bit if the dramatic change in subject made him look like a jerk.

She made a cute noise, half-laugh half-cough. "Me? How about you? I just bounce. All women can bounce. It's a prerequisite to having kids and bouncing them to sleep. But you? I've never known a man to dance and not look like a fool. You did not look like a fool."

He glanced at her then, and she was smiling. He loved the way the expression lifted her cheeks into perfect round balls. "Thanks, but it's no great feat. When you come from a family as big as mine, you go to a lot of weddings."

And funerals. Those horrid memories lingered. And that was the problem. Life was a pinball game of weddings and funerals, bouncing from one to the other, throwing in a christening here and there. At the moment, not a single unattached Corcarelli was ready to marry, which meant the next bumper he'd hit was a funeral. Nonna's funeral.

His brain mashed the thoughts into a wayward image of Nonna at the last family wedding. She beamed while Father Joe blessed the unholy union of Vin and Carrie. Even Nonna knew the relationship was shaky, but she smiled anyway, content with the priest's proclamation that the pair was a couple before God and man. Hokey if you asked Tony, especially since the marriage was annulled three months later. But considering what was happening now with Nonna's cancer, he was sort of thankful for Vin's mistake. That wedding gave Nonna great joy.

If only Tony could find his own Carrie. Not that he wanted to be married to a gold digger. Not that he had much gold to give. But a woman who had no intention of staying married to him, a woman who would eagerly let him off the hook three months after giving Nonna the biggest thrill of what was left of her life? Yeah, Tony could use one of those.

Problem was, where to find her on such short notice.

• • •

Trish looked at Tony, holding open the passenger side door, and then to the lighted front porch of her house. She wanted to get out of the car. She knew she should get out of the car, put some distance between her and the subject of her crazy idea. But her body wouldn't move. It was as if every cell of her being knew this was her best shot.

At what? Insanity? Trish balked.

"You sure you don't want to talk about it?" He leaned an elbow on the top of the car door and tipped his head to the right. Moonlight sparkled in his hair and eyes.

"I'm sure." There was no way she wanted to talk about him being the father of her baby. Thinking about talking about it was bad enough. She swung her legs around and planted her heels on the pavement.

His gaze followed. Instead of the usual inappropriate comment, he simply smiled and backed away, giving her room to stand.

Now what? Shake his hand and skitter away? Hug him? The thought of him holding her close like he did on the dance floor had her nerves dropping like dead weight into the pit of her stomach.

"Thanks again, Tony." She flashed a quick smile and brushed by him, hoping her quickstep up the walk didn't look as foolish as it felt.

When she stopped on the porch to gather her keys, she heard footsteps on the wooden stairs behind her.

"You didn't have to walk me to the door," she said, spinning around to face him.

He grinned. "Yes, I did. A Corcarelli man is taught never to shirk his duties. Escorting a woman to the safety of her front door is one of them. Besides, I promised your father I would get you home safely."

She nodded. "Honorable." And then she dropped her head and her attention to the bottom of her purse, because her thoughts were anything but. The minute he'd mentioned his struggles with Nonna's wish list, and Nonna's desire for him to marry and have kids, Trish's brain started concocting a plan.

"In this instance, yes. I'm being honorable."

"In every instance I've ever witnessed you in," she chattered as she pushed aside a tube of lipstick and a travel pack of tissues. She wasn't even sure what she was chattering about. She only hoped the conversation would keep things cordial without him asking something stupid like could he come in, because she'd say yes, and then she'd end up propositioning him—and not in the usual way. Nope, there was nothing usual about asking a man to father her child—so he could make his grandmother's wish come true, while he made Trish's wish come true, too.

"You haven't witnessed me in many places outside work. That's where I run into trouble."

"It's all in good fun, I'm sure." She wrapped her hand around the silver key and yanked it from her purse. In her overzealousness, the key clanged to the porch floorboards.

Tony sunk on a bend of his knees and gathered what she'd dropped. When he stood, he leaned past her and slid the key into the deadbolt lock. With a flick of his wrist, the door fanned open.

"There," he said, lifting her right hand palm up where he could deposit the key. He cradled her hand while his fingertips pressed into her palm around the cool metal.

"Thank you," she stammered.

"Don't mention it."

There was something else she shouldn't mention, something that bit at the tip of her tongue. As she fought with the words, she stared up at his handsome face, noticing how his dark eyes and brows reminded her of Angie's, but how his wider nose twisted the familial resemblance into a unique, masculine edge.

"Do you want to come in?" Somehow Trish managed not to cringe. Apparently a wandering mind led to loose lips.

Tony opened his mouth, and his shoulders rose and fell. "I want to do a lot of things I shouldn't. That tends to be what gets me labeled as the black sheep of my family."

He was still holding her hand, but the pressure of his fingertips had lightened until the tickle to her palm caused by the vague movement of a simple breath had her hanging on his answer. "Is that a yes or a no?"

With a grin, he closed her fingers around the key and dropped her hand. "I think I better get the car back to Vin."

Disappointment throttled the hope his grin had created. "Okay."

His brows furrowed, and she wondered if the disappointment showed on her face.

"You wouldn't want to come with me, would you?" he asked, his brows still knotted above his nose, like he wasn't at all certain he should be asking the question in the first place.

Trish made a quick mental list of her options, which included heading to bed—alone—or prolonging her evening with Tony. "Yes," she said.

"It would involve riding my bike home."

She looked down at her dress. "I'm not sure I can ride in this."

"I saw you dance in that, remember." He winked. "If you can grind, you can ride."

Before she could do something about the recklessness taking over her normally practical mind, Tony reached out to close her front door. He took the key from her hand, locked the house, and then pulled her off the front porch.

"Don't tell Angie," he said. His quick smile gave Trish the feeling he was only partly joking.

"I won't." She slid back onto the passenger seat and let him close the door behind her.

Her brain echoed the mantra *what am I doing*. Her heart was afraid of the answer. Regardless, by the time the sun came up she knew she was going to take this thing with Tony too far.

CHAPTER SIX

Vin's gated riverside condo complex glowed beneath the sparkle of a cloudless sky. Tony admired the stars and the perfect night for riding. That sky was the best reason yet to ditch this car. Not that the car wasn't great. Not that Tony wasn't thankful for the loan. But the car came with too much responsibility to keep it scratch-free—and too much room in the single row of seats. More than once on the five-mile drive from Trish's house to Vin's condo, he'd entertained thoughts of stretching her lush body along these vintage leather seats.

Clearly the night wasn't going to end until he did something stupid. The least he could do was not involve Vin's precious car.

After snaking his way to the back of the complex and the river's edge, Tony hit the button on the garage opener and guided the car into the empty spot next to his beloved bike. With any luck Vin wouldn't come sniffing around for damage until Tony and Trish were long gone.

Tony put the car in park just as the door to the house opened. Vin stepped into the garage, wearing nothing but a pair of basketball shorts and a scowl, and he was looking right at Trish.

"He looks angry," she mumbled.

"You've seen him at enough family functions to know he always looks angry. Ignore him." Tony pushed out of the car and smiled at Vin. "I brought her home in one piece."

"I see that," Vin leered, looking from Trish to Tony and back to Trish again.

"Not a mark on her."

"Yet." Vin stared at Tony a second longer, and then dropped his searing gaze to inspect his car.

"Hi, Vin. Nice to see you again. Great car." Trish's voice wobbled. She stood between the car and Tony's bike, wringing her hands like a teenager caught by her father during a driveway make out session. Flushed cheeks. Sparkling eyes. Gnawed bottom lip. It was a great look on her.

"Tony," Vin barked.

"Yeah," Tony answered, turning his face from Trish to the drill sergeant in the doorway.

"How 'bout you come inside and get your keys." He tossed a curt nod to Trish and disappeared into the condo.

Tony smiled at her.

"Are you in trouble?" she asked, a crooked grin on her reddened face.

"Probably. Wait here. I'll be right back."

When Tony walked into the condo, he came face to face with Vin. "You are a fucking moron."

Tony nodded. "Thanks for the compliment. Now give me my keys."

"Not if you're going to take them and drive that lady anywhere else but to her home, where you will leave her the hell alone."

"I appreciate your concern." Despite the itch he had to deck Vin for the self-righteous lecture, Tony smiled and held out his hand.

Vin dropped the keys in Tony's palm, but then quick as lightning, strangled his wrist. "Appreciate this. Ange will skin you alive if she knows you're messing with her best friend."

Tony ripped his hand free. "Thanks for the car, Vin." He stormed out of the condo before things got ugly.

Not convinced Vin wouldn't follow to embarrass Tony by lecturing in front of Trish, Tony half-sprinted to the bike, where she waited.

"I don't know how to do this." She looked pale.

He didn't have time to put her fears to rest. Shrugging out of his suit coat, he tossed it at her. "Put that on. It's gonna get cold." Then he grabbed the handlebars and tossed his right leg over the seat, walking the bike backward out of the garage until he was facing forward in the driveway.

He waved Trish to his side, and when she was close enough, he snatched her arm, pulling her to him. "It's simple. Straddle the seat, plaster your boobs against my back, and hang the hell on."

He fired up the bike before she—or Vin—could say a word.

Seconds later, the full weight of her upper body pressed against his back as he rocketed off, shattering the evening silence. Vin was right. Tony was going to pay for all the wicked things he wanted to do to Trish, starting with running his hand up her stockings so he could feel how high her dress rode up her thighs.

Maybe the urgency to misbehave grew on the harshness of Vin's warning or the rushing crush of cold air against Tony's face. More than likely it was Trish's chin resting on his shoulder and the heat from her hands, clinging to his pecs. Whatever the reason, as he slowed his speed amid city traffic, he reached behind him to find her. Hooking his hand beneath her knee, he soaked in the soft but ragged feel of fishnet, and then moved his hand higher along the outside of her thigh. All the while her hands pressed deeper into his chest, until he could feel the bite of her fingernails.

But then traffic opened up, and Tony needed both hands on the bars to keep control of the bike.

Trish's hands never let up with the pressure. Even when he cut the motor in front of her house, she choked his chest. He wasn't sure if it was shock from his hand's impromptu exploration or fear from his driving. Either way, he was a little worried to face her.

Her hot, staccato breaths tickled the side of his neck, and his shoulder muscle throbbed beneath the weight of her chin. Such a strange combination of pleasure and pain. Strange enough to hold him there, savoring the sensations.

"Now what?" she whispered.

He patted her rigged hands. "You need to get off." The words didn't sound nearly as filthy as they tasted.

"Oh. Okay." She slid her hands around his chest and released his shoulder from the piercing pressure of her chin. Then she clamped onto his shoulders and pushed against him until he couldn't feel her anymore.

He didn't like the icy feel of that one bit.

When he dropped his right foot to the ground, he glanced behind him, so as not to kick her with his left leg when he swung off the bike. She stood out of reach, tugging her dress beneath his unbuttoned suit coat to her bended knees. Her blonde hair, battered from the wind, fell in clumps around her face, hiding her eyes, but he could see her teeth pulling at her bottom lip, and he had a clear shot of some impressive cleavage.

Damn, he liked his women muddled.

Lust punched a hole in his gut and yanked him off the bike. When he came to a stop in front of her, she froze. Hands flat on her belly, knees still bent. "You okay?" he asked.

She tipped her head slightly and regarded him with shiny eyes. "You don't wear a helmet?"

"It's not against the law in Pennsylvania."

"I know, but what about protection?" She straightened, and when she did, his coat slipped from her right shoulder.

She was a glorious mess, so unlike the professional, capable Trish DeVign he knew.

Tony reached for her, slipping his hand to her arm and pinching the coat between his fingers, dragging it over her smooth skin. Heat tightened his belly.

"Sometimes protection is overrated," he whispered. "Sometimes all it does is get in the way of the experience."

She slapped a hand over her mouth and backed away.

Shit. Now he'd done it. He'd shocked the hell out of her. Any minute she'd turn and run.

Eyes wide, she dropped her hand. "You've pushed me to this, Tony. I have no choice."

He raised his palms to her, hoping to stop the tumble, wanting to fix things enough to save him from losing his livelihood and facing Angie's wrath. "I'm sorry. I…"

"We should have a baby together." Trish slapped her hand over her mouth again.

Tony fidgeted in the eerie silence, and then stuffed a finger into his ear, digging around like maybe he'd heard her wrong. But was there any mistaking those words? "I'm not sure how to respond to that."

She covered her eyes with her hands. "I know," she whined. "Go ahead. Say it. I'm insane." With a giant inhale, she threw her arms out to her side and slapped her palms to her head. In a blink her arms dropped to her sides and her hands disappeared into the sleeves of his suit coat. "I've been thinking about this, planning this a long time, but nothing prepared me for how ridiculous it would sound when I said it out loud."

Okay, now he was worried. Maybe something happened on the back of the bike. Maybe she had been hit on the head. "You've been thinking about having a baby…with me…for a long time?"

She gave her head a crazy shake, one that further loosened the hair from its knot. "No. I only started thinking about having a baby with you earlier tonight, but I've been thinking about having a baby for two years now." She exhaled. "Listen, I don't expect you to fully understand. You can't. You're not adopted. You have blood relatives living on practically every block in Pittsburgh. But I don't. I don't have any. And I want one, only one. That's all I'm asking for." She rolled back her shoulders and lifted her chin. "Tony, I don't want your money. I don't want your undying love. I just want your sperm…and your family. In return, I'll help you make one of Nonna's wishes come true." Air sputtered from her lips as she dropped her head.

Damn. She was serious—or at least she thought she was serious. Either way, he couldn't bolt, which was what the pea-sized, rational part of his brain was screaming for him to do. He owed her the chance to explain—or at least to talk herself out of the craziness.

He stared at the top of her head, trying to determine his next move. All he could think was how he expected tonight to hold a proposition. He just never expected a proposition like this.

. . .

Trish wanted to drop to her knees and dig a hole where she could bury herself along with her ludicrous ideas. Any man in his right mind would run, but not before he tried to convince her to admit herself for observation at the nearest psychiatric unit.

She saw the tips of Tony's dress shoes before she saw his hand, reaching for hers.

"Can we have this conversation inside?" He laced his fingers with hers and pulled her hand to his chest. "If I have relatives on every block in Pittsburgh, one of them is bound to see us. Can you imagine the rumors?"

She lifted her head and spit out a laugh. "Yeah, well the rumors can't be half as crazy as the truth."

Still he was smiling that crooked, heart-swelling grin that got her into this mess in the first place.

"Come on," he said, tossing his head toward the door and tugging on her hand until she had no choice but to follow.

They walked the flagstone path in silence, giving Trish plenty of time to rehash her stupidity. But with her hand warmed in his, it was hard not to be hopeful. Maybe the idea wasn't as crazy as it seemed.

At the top of the porch steps, they stopped, and Tony faced her. "Key." He pointed to her left breast.

Trish looked at his finger, lightly touching the black fabric of his suit coat she was still wearing, and then he flipped the lapel and slipped his hand inside the pocket, all the while brushing her breast with the back of his hand.

The moment was over in two blinks, but her goose-pimpled skin lingered.

"After you," he said, opening the front door, releasing her hand and stepping aside.

She walked into her house, stopping in the foyer, staring at the black tips of her shoes, listening to the door closing behind them.

"Point me to the kitchen. I'll make you some tea."

"Tea?" She turned around on the random offer.

Tony shrugged. "People in distress always drink tea on TV." His crooked smile didn't take the edge off the word "distress."

"I'm not distressed, Tony, and I don't want tea."

"Okay." He shoved his hands into his pockets and inhaled enough to raise his chest against the cool blue of his dress shirt. He looked bigger and stronger than she remembered, and at the moment she wished she'd never mentioned a baby.

"I'm sorry, Tony."

"Listen, Trish. I'm the one who should be apologizing. You're right. I pushed you. All those insinuations. The motorcycle ride. The hand up your leg…" His eyes darkened along with the dip in his cheek. "Yeah. I crossed the line."

Maybe, but it was a line that needed to be crossed by someone if she ever wanted to have a baby. She'd spent two years so concerned with finding the appropriate candidate she never let her guard down enough to feel half the desire Tony elicited from her during one non-date.

She cleared the nerves from her throat. She could do this. She sold her ideas to hundreds of clients every year. This didn't have to be any different. "I really hope you'll consider crossing that line again, but first," she clasped her hands in front of her, "hear me out."

He raised one beautiful black brow.

"In the living room," she said, walking away from him, hoping he'd follow.

A rush of adrenaline boosted her confidence when she didn't hear the front door open and close. *I can do this*, she thought over and over again.

Stepping into the living room, she stopped on the edge of a blood red Persian rug and slipped his coat from her arms, letting it fall below her backside, hoping Tony still liked what he saw when he looked at her. Of course, hers wasn't the usual seduction with success being a quick trip to bed. She had exactly one shot to convince this man that she was worth the trouble it would take to get her pregnant.

Trish cringed. She was an idiot.

With a sigh, she faced him and held out his coat. "I'm good. You can have this back."

He reached for the jacket with a smile. "I can't figure you out."

"Just wait." She walked to the sofa and sat, mostly because her feet hurt and her knees were weak, but partly because she expected him to leave her disappointed, and the sofa would make the perfect place to brood. "So here goes." She sucked a mouthful of air and shot it right back out her mouth. "I'm adopted."

"You said that." He walked to the chair closest to her and sat, crossing his ankle over his knee, draping the suit coat across his lap.

"I want a baby."

"You said that too."

"Tony, stop interrupting me. This is hard enough."

He grinned, nodded and propped his elbows on the arms of the chair, bringing his fingers to his lips. He was so embarrassingly attractive, the idea of making a baby with him had her toes curling in her shoes and heat creeping up her face.

She looked to the brilliant white crown molding over his head. "A couple years ago I decided time was running out, and if I wanted to ever have a baby I was going to have to make it a major focus. When I wasn't working on my other major focus—design—I was systematically dating prospective husbands and fathers. I know that sounds desperate and terribly unromantic, but I tend to be a methodical person." Tony chuckled. Trish gave him the stink eye. "Anyhow, that didn't work so well. Everyone fell short."

"Except me." He grinned.

"Shush." She would not let that grin rattle her. "I thought about a sperm bank." Her cheeks heated again. "But not knowing either of my biological parents, it's important to me that my child knows both of his or hers. So it was back to dating, only this time I didn't care about finding a husband. My sole focus was to find a man I could have a baby with. No strings, really. Except I hoped he'd be willing to see the child a couple times a year. After Jackson likened having kids to having surgery without anesthesia, I was starting to give up hope, but then…"

"Me." He rested his folded hands in his lap.

"You." Trish nodded. "All the talk about Nonna's list, and your comment about wanting kids but not the marriage. And…the chemistry between us." She studied the crown molding again. "I had to ask. You may be my best shot."

"I'm flattered."

"But you still think I'm crazy."

"No, I get why you want a baby, and I respect that you've given it a lot of thought."

"But you don't want to have a baby with me."

He laughed, stood and crossed the carpet to settle on the sofa beside her where he wrapped his hands around hers. "There's still more to think about."

"Like?"

His thumbs traced tiny circles on her knuckles. "What'll Ange say about this?"

Trish managed a painful swallow as she watched Tony's thumbs swirl. She wished the luscious sensation of being held in his hands outweighed the sickening sensation of imagining Angie's reaction to the news. "She wasn't happy I asked you to the wedding."

"Exactly. Vin wasn't happy either. We could screw up a lot here, Trish."

She knew that, but she knew something else, too. "Think of Nonna, Tony." Trish squeezed his hands. "And what if we had a son? We could do a lot of good here, too."

CHAPTER SEVEN

Tony didn't think Trish was crazy, but he might be. Sitting on the couch beside her with the proposition floating between them, he was 99 percent in favor of having a baby with her. It would certainly solve his problem of what big, happy contribution he could make to Nonna's wish list. And heck, he wasn't getting any younger. Thirty-three wasn't old, but if he waited for the urge to do things the traditional way, it would be too late.

He glanced at her, studying the palms of her hands. She slid a stack of silver rings up and down her index finger. If he was going to have a child with anyone, she'd be a good choice, not because of any romantic notions, but because he liked her, respected her, knew she'd raise a child right, which in Tony's opinion meant lots of love and security. If her business and friendships were any indication, Trish DeVign didn't do anything halfway.

And heck, she was gorgeous. Making a kid with her was bound to create a perfect human specimen. Still, it wasn't an easy decision. There were…logistics. Whens and hows. Not that he didn't know how to get a woman pregnant, but Trish was the designer of this plan, maybe she wanted to handle things medically rather than the old-fashioned way.

Tony liked the old-fashioned way.

He leaned forward, resting his elbows on his widened knees. "You said you've been thinking about this for a long time, got it all planned out. How exactly did you imagine making this baby?"

She squirmed on the cushion beside him, shoving her folded hands between her locked thighs. "The usual way."

Tony smiled.

"I'm totally clean," she continued. "I can get paperwork from my doctor as proof. I was just there…to make sure, so you don't have to worry about that. Of course, I'd want verification that you're good, too. Oh, and you don't have to worry about knocking my socks off or anything. It's purely clinical. Tactical. You know?"

No. He didn't. He hadn't had sex in the purely clinical sense since he was seventeen. He wasn't sure he could go back to that, even if he wanted to. "That's a bummer. You said we had chemistry."

"We do."

"Then what makes you think we can't have a little fun while we make a baby?"

She shrugged. "I'm a little uptight when I'm trying to achieve something." She looked everywhere but him, pulling her bottom lip between rows of perfect teeth.

He chuckled. "Are we talking baby or orgasm here?"

The red of her cheeks matched the red stripe on her walls. "Both," she squeaked.

He squeezed her knee. "Trust me. You would be in good hands—on both accounts."

Either the contact or the words made her jump, and her jump made Tony wonder how she'd ever relax enough to actually go through with her plan.

He straightened and angled his body to her. "We need to sleep on this." She opened her mouth and sucked in a breath. "In separate beds," he added with a smile. "I need to go home. You need to stay here. And we need to think some more before we act."

She nodded. "I suppose that's best."

"If we do this thing, we're going to have to spend a lot of time together to convince my family it's real. I'll piss them off if it looks like I'm just messing around with you."

But truth be told, messing around with Trish hadn't left his mind since he laid eyes on her in those fishnet stockings. And to think he was this close to a free pass.

He slipped a hand to her face, cradling her soft cheek, loving how she responded, dropping her chin and resting against him. "Good night," he whispered, pulling her face gently to him as he leaned in and placed a chaste kiss on her forehead. "I'll call you tomorrow."

He stood, snatched his coat off a nearby chair and walked into the hall.

"Thank you, Tony."

He stopped with his hand on the front door knob. "For what?"

"For not thinking I'm crazy." She lifted a hand and brushed a clump of hair off her face, tucking it behind her ear, letting her fingers rest at the back of her neck. With her head tilted and her lower lip drawn between her teeth, she looked nervous, but her blue eyes sparkled with determination. There it was again, that irresistible blend that made Trish unique and Tony interested.

He had to remind himself it wasn't smart for him to stay until they both had more time to think things through. With a smile and a twist of the knob, he stepped outside. "Lock this door behind me."

"Okay." She raised a thin brow and wrapped her arms around her waist. The motion deepened her cleavage.

Tony stood on the porch, toes touching the metal threshold separating wooden slats from slate title. "Whatever you do, don't let me back in."

She dropped her arms and walked those wicked legs in his direction, stopping just inside the foyer, toes touching the metal threshold too. "Don't let you back in ever?"

"Just tonight."

"Ah." Her lips hitched as she nodded. "Chemistry, right?"

"Absolutely," he answered, stepping backward so as not to get caught up in the tractor beam pull. Not yet, anyway. He had a lot of thinking to do.

• • •

The next morning, Tony squatted beside the bench seat he'd removed from Angie's Cadillac, hoping that working on Angie's project would take his mind off Trish's project—that one kept him up all night. If he wasn't thinking about how much fun he'd have making a baby with Trish, he was thinking about how much fun he'd have being a father. But when he stripped away the thoughts of fun, he was left with a couple concerns, like how fast could a woman get pregnant, and how long did Nonna have to live?

He knew the basics about pregnancy. He knew how to make it happen. He knew babies baked for nine months. But he didn't know if Nonna had nine months to live. No one did. He'd seen her a handful of times since the diagnosis, and she didn't look any different to him. Sadder maybe, but not sick. Even the doctors couldn't be pinned to a timeframe, and chemo and radiation could change the course of things. All Tony knew for sure was that if he wanted this baby to bring joy to Nonna, then the faster he could get Trish pregnant, the better. So what was stopping him?

He scraped a palm over the stubble on his left cheek and reached for an electric carving knife, hoping the mindless motion of cutting foam would put his worries to rest, but before he could flip the switch, a bang vibrated the garage walls.

"Grinding?"

"Excuse me?" Tony didn't look in Angie's direction.

"What were you thinking, Tony? Grinding with Trish!"

He looked then, more than a little surprised his sister had details about last night this early in the a.m. "She told you?"

"No, Piper Betts couldn't wait to tell me. She's keyboardist in that jazz band."

"Oh," he said, sitting back on his heels, oddly relived that Trish hadn't been the one to spill the beans about their dirty dancing.

How would they ever pull this baby thing off if she was blabbing gory details to Angie? "I didn't see Piper there."

"Of course you didn't. You were too busy grinding against my best friend."

"So what?" He shrugged and turned his attention to the foam, picking lint from the yellow rectangle.

"You must've mortified her. DeVigns don't grind."

The image of Trish in fishnet stockings dropping low to the ground as she smoothed her ass against him burned a hole through his brain. "Yeah? Well, you're misinformed. Trish is a mighty fine grinder."

Something scratchy but moist hit him square in the forehead. "Hey." He looked at the carwash sponge Angie had pitched at his head. "What was that for?"

"Don't fuck with her, Tony." When he looked up, he saw Angie holding a ball peen hammer in her hand. He knew better than to worry she would throw that, too, but it sure gave her an ominous edge. "Trish is not for hire in your harem. She's kind and sincere, and you'll break her heart."

'Cause in Angie's eyes that was all he ever did—love 'em and leave 'em. Angie didn't get that these things could be mutual. "Trish is a big girl," he said, snatching the carwash sponge from the foam and tossing it to the garage floor.

"Damn it, Tony. I'm serious. There's not a sincere bone in your body, unless you count the one in your pants. And I don't. Leave Trish alone. I don't want to be cleaning up another one of your messes, especially if it involves my friend."

Back to this again. Angie considered manning Dad's carpentry company "cleaning up" one of Tony's messes. If only he'd been responsible enough to do the right thing and follow in the old man's footsteps, Angie would be the one running around carefree. Or not. She wasn't exactly the carefree type. Whatever. If she wanted to blame him for her moodiness, so be it. Nothing new. And she was probably right to be warning him off Trish.

Tony switched on the electric knife. He could only imagine what Angie would say if she knew the extent of the mess he was considering creating with her best friend. Cutting into the foam, he relaxed and reminded himself he hadn't done anything stupid yet.

There was still a glimmer of hope for him.

• • •

When Trish heard the bell over the front door chime, she looked up from the media room sketch she'd been battling all morning. Angie walked toward Trish's desk, keeping to the natural aisle formed between a row of model furniture and a line of floral accents. She wasn't dressed for work, and her face was missing a smile.

"Hey, you," Trish said brightly, despite the nerves picking at her neck. It was awkward seeing Angie so soon after what transpired last night with Tony. "Did we have a meeting scheduled?"

"No, but I'm thinking we should talk." Angie's nose crinkled and her nostrils flared.

"What's up?" Upon inhaling, Trish sucked the words right back into the pit of her upset stomach. Angie was on to her.

"Piper Betts saw you grinding with my brother."

"Who's Piper Betts, and since when did we return to middle school?" Trish laughed, hoping to keep the conversation light and not incriminating.

Angie dropped onto the Lucite chair opposite from Trish's desk. "Piper's an old friend. She plays in the band that played at your cousin's wedding."

"Oh." Trish rolled her pencil and three markers off the paper in front of her, settling them on the desk.

"That's all you have to say for yourself?"

"Ange, it's no big deal."

"*Yet.* When Tony's involved, it can go from no big deal to raging mess in under five seconds."

If Angie only knew. "You say that, but…" Trish remembered how caring and understanding Tony had been. Surely if he was the jerk Angie made him out to be, he wouldn't have walked away from the opportunity to sleep with Trish last night. "I need more proof."

"What?"

"I need proof that Tony's capable of the messes you're always talking about. Honestly, I don't see it."

"Holy shit." Angie stood. "Did you sleep with him?"

Trish's cheeks ignited. "No." But not for lack of wanting.

"He's going to hurt you."

"How so?"

"What do you mean, how so? I know you! You want marriage. Kids. Tony thinks marriage is for losers who can't get laid on a regular basis without the gold band, and he's too much of a kid himself to raise one."

Funny, as much as Trish loved Angie, she was getting tired of the slams against Tony's character. "Maybe you don't know me as well as you think. Maybe I want a little fun now and then, too."

Crap. Angie's face twisted like Trish's gut did. "I'm sorry, Ange. I didn't mean you didn't know me. You know me. You…"

"Forget it. Whatever. Tony's right. You're a big girl. But I warned you. Remember that." She turned and walked away.

"Ange, wait." Trish jumped up and ran after her. If she wanted to have a baby with Tony, she was going to have to get used to smoothing wrinkles between her and Angie. "I like Tony, and if that makes me an idiot, then I take full responsibility."

Angie stopped and turned. "Fine."

"So you're okay with it…with me liking him?"

"No, but what am I going to do about it? I love him. I love you. It's not like I can give up on either one of you."

That made Trish smile, and some of the stress she'd been carrying around all morning evaporated. "I'm going to hug you now."

"Don't." Angie put out both arms. "I hurt my back carrying boards. You'll make it worse."

"Liar." Trish sidestepped the outstretched arms and wrapped Angie in a fierce hug. "I love you, too."

"Oh God. Too much. Too much," Angie said, squirming.

But when Trish released her, Angie was smiling. "I'm serious, Ange. You'll never know how much your friendship means to me."

"That's all I need to know. Don't tell me more. It'll just lead to hugging." She pointed a finger at Trish's face. "And another thing you better not be telling me...details about you and my brother doing whatever you end up doing. I do not want to know. Got me?"

"Loud and clear," Trish answered with a nod, because, frankly, she couldn't agree more. If Angie knew details of what Trish and Tony were thinking about doing, there'd be hell to pay, hell in the form of ruthless lectures and character smearing meant to change Trish's mind. More than likely, when faced with that kind of pressure from Angie, Trish would crumble. Under those circumstances, she wouldn't choose a baby with Tony over her best friend. But if Trish happened to get pregnant while she was doing whatever she and Tony ended up doing—details Angie refused to hear—there'd be no choice to make. Trish would get to have her baby and keep her best friend, too.

"Why are you looking at me so weird?" Angie narrowed her eyes.

Trish released an anxious laugh. "No reason. Get out of here. I have sketches to finish."

Angie nodded as she walked out of the shop, glancing back at Trish every so often like she was suspicious. Trish waved through the glass, partly to keep up appearances and partly to release nervous energy. She wouldn't be settled until she was pregnant, because then the damage would be done, and she'd be mere months away from her greatest dream coming true.

When Angie turned the corner, Trish released a big breath. As tough as it was, she laid the groundwork by letting Angie know she was interested in Tony. Now all Trish needed was for Tony to be interested in her.

• • •

Tony parallel parked his bike between a dumpster and Ma's Accord. He tossed a few stray cans into the dumpster and then ducked into the narrow space between houses to get to the side door. He knocked and at the same time saw Ma sitting at the kitchen table, piles of pictures in her hands.

"Come in," she mouthed.

So he did. Closing the door behind him, he stepped into the kitchen, sucked a lungful of warm, oven-scented air and walked to her side. "Where's Nonna?" He kissed the top of her head.

"Napping in the spare bedroom. She only made it through the first dozen cookies today. The cancer makes her tired."

Tony nodded, ignoring the pinch of worry in his gut. Just because Nonna was extra tired didn't mean she was dying soon.

"What's this?" he asked, gesturing to the mess of pictures on the table.

"Father Campbell has the RCIA class making collages of what inspired us to become Catholic."

Tony picked up a nearby picture of his father, holding the same ball peen hammer Angie had shaken earlier. Pasquale Corcarelli was standing outside this very house with a giant smile on his face, a smile that looked an awful lot like the one Tony saw every time he looked at pictures of himself. He reached for one of those, too, holding the photographs side by side.

"You look so much like him." Ma wrapped an arm around Tony's waist and leaned her head against his hip.

Tony transferred both pictures to his right hand and patted Ma's shoulder with his left. "I know I do." But that was where the similarities ended.

"I should've done this for him. My biggest regret is not becoming Catholic while he was alive. I thought I was keeping the peace between my father and him by staying a Methodist, but any peace I managed shattered when I agreed to have you and Angie raised Catholic. Still..." She reached up and squeezed Tony's hand, resting on her shoulder. "I spent the rest of my father's life trying to make up for disappointing him, and in the process I missed celebrating with you. Never once did I fully partake in a sacrament. I couldn't relax enough to be happy for the spiritual gifts my own children were being given." She patted his hand as she shook her head. "Well, not anymore. After these classes, I can celebrate with my grandchildren." When she looked at him, pressure popped in Tony's head.

Ma didn't know about Trish's plan. She couldn't know. And yet, she was a mother. Mothers had that sixth sense, didn't they?

Tony pulled out the chair beside her and sat. "I took Trish DeVign to her cousin's wedding yesterday." Maybe he was looking to confess, to be saved from making another mess Angie would have to clean.

Ma set the piles of pictures down and looked him over. "Did you have a nice time?"

Tony scanned the pictures scattered around the table. "Yeah, I did," he said, nodding.

"Is this more than a casual favor sort of thing?"

"I think it's headed that way." Despite his reservations and the confrontation with Angie in her garage, something about Trish's proposal made sense to him. "I don't think Ange is happy about it, though."

"She doesn't like to be put in the middle."

"Nobody's putting her there."

Ma grabbed his hands.

"Be careful, Tony. Trisha's a good girl." She reached up and patted his cheek. "You're a good boy, too. One of these days you're going to stop beating yourself up for being who you are, and you're going to let somebody love you the right way, the way you deserve to be loved."

He patted his hand on top of hers. "Yeah, Ma, that's what you keep saying."

"Mark my word. I'm going to be taking communion at your wedding." And when she smiled, Tony knew this plan of Trish's could make one more dream come true.

He didn't often find himself in the position to bring so much joy to so many people. The thought percolated until it overflowed his brain and attached to his heart.

"I gotta go, Ma." Tony patted her hand once more and then pushed back in the chair to stand.

"Well, that was a short visit."

He snatched a couple *pizzelles* off the counter. "I came to see Nonna...and for these...and of course, to see you. But since she's napping and you're busy, I'll leave you in peace." He came for clarity too, and boy, did he find it.

Now he needed to find the guts to follow through.

CHAPTER EIGHT

Trish shook Mrs. Davenport's hand and led her to the front of the store. "I won't place the fabric order until tomorrow, so if you have second thoughts between now and then, let me know."

"I'm sure it will look wonderful." The middle-aged woman twisted a floral scarf around her neck and pushed her shoulder against the leaded glass door. "We'll talk soon."

Trish smiled, nodded and watched her leave. Checking the silver watch dangling from her left wrist, she figured she had enough time to make at least one phone call before her meeting with the tile rep.

Back behind her desk, she glanced at her cell phone. Tony said he'd call. He hadn't. Maybe he wouldn't. Two days was plenty of time to come to his senses and see her for the control freak she was. Who proposed something like this, having a baby with her best friend's brother? Trish's shoulders slumped, but then she lifted her chin and righted her posture. *No moping.* There was decorating to do.

The door chimed, and Trish glanced toward the sound, hoping the tile rep wasn't early.

"Hey, Boss Lady." Tony strode down the shop aisle like a vision conjured by her obsessive brain.

A plaid oxford rolled up at the sleeves opened over a black T-shirt. Battered and beaten gray jeans hung beltless from his hips. And he was wearing boots, black boots, scuffed at the toes. No polish, no refinement, could ever look that good.

"Hi." She waved, lifting her left hand and flicking her wrist. "What's up?" Dumb question. She was trying too hard to sound flippant, and she didn't need a mirror to tell her she wasn't matching his picture of cool.

"I've been thinking, and I bet you have been, too."

For a split second she thought to play coy, to make him spell out his thoughts, at least to delay the inevitable awkwardness of rehashing their conversation. But, if she ever hoped to have a baby, she needed to suck it up and face the sensitive subject matter. This was not an easy conversation or decision, and a "yes" wouldn't magically take the weirdness away.

"I've been thinking a lot too…" she managed a small smile, "wondering if you've finally come to your senses and realized I was crazy or if you maybe, sorta, kinda want what I want, too."

He walked around the desk and stood beside her, grinning. "Let's just say I'm willing to explore the opportunity."

His silky voice acted like a summons to the butterflies locked in her gut. They fluttered against her ribs, quickening her heart. "What does that mean exactly?"

He reached behind him into his back pocket, drawing his jeans lower on his right hip, and then he presented her with a folded sheet of thin white paper. "Should we proceed, you'll want this."

"What is it?"

"Take a look."

Trish scanned the lab report, which proved Tony was clean. The realization that she was one step closer to making a baby with him acted like a vacuum in her head, sucking out thought and function, leaving her more than a little light-headed. She drew a breath and closed her eyes, hoping to maintain her balance.

He grabbed her hand, laced his fingers with hers, and held her straight. "You okay?"

When she looked at him, he wasn't smiling, but there was something comforting about his face. Concern, maybe. Sincerity. She wasn't sure. But whatever it was made her tossing insides halt their churn. "I am. I guess I'm nervous, which seems strange, because I was so sure about this for so long."

"You're not sure now?"

"No. No. I am. Definitely. It's just more awkward than I thought it would be."

"Because you're taking all the fun out of it." His thumb circled the knuckle on her index finger. "You need to relax."

"I know. Stress can inhibit pregnancy, and that's the last thing I want to do. It's just that every time I..."

He lifted her knuckles to his lips, stopping her words cold. "I can help you relax." Back and forth, he smoothed the soft surface of his mouth over the bumps on her hand until she had to bite her lip to keep from whimpering. "How's that? Better?"

Trish nodded. "A little."

"You want me to up my game?"

She couldn't imagine what upping his game would entail, and she couldn't imagine how she'd survive it, because his mouth exploring the surface of her hand was enough to weaken her knees. "No, I'm good."

He raised his brows and stared at her over the top of her hand, which was still pressed to his mouth. "Good." And then he lifted his head away from her hand, but didn't release her. "How long do you think it will take to get pregnant?"

"I, um..." She had to push the word past the lump in her throat. "I'm pretty regular, if you catch my drift. I've been charting for over a year now so I was ready if...when...you know."

He grinned. "I know." And then he sat on her desk, wrapped his free hand around her waist, and slid her to him.

Her feet stuffed between his. "Tony, what are you doing?"

With his body weight on the edge of her desk and her body weight on the soles of her riding boots, there was plenty of space between them. "Testing you out. Getting a feel for the goods." He hitched his lip. "You can't expect me to go into this cold."

She pushed against his chest. "Funny."

"Then why aren't you laughing?"

"I'm at work, Tony. When I'm at work, I'm all business."

He grinned. "Yeah. I like that about you, so serious." The last word came deeper and slower than the rest.

She pushed him again. "You're mocking me."

"No, I'm helping you relax. Remember?"

"Yes, well, this is a serious subject." She crinkled her face and tried to step out of his space.

He held her there. "You think I don't know that? Yeah, it's serious, and if we don't find the fun in it, we're both going to end up running off with cold feet."

God, she couldn't bear the thought. Not when she was this close, closer than she'd ever been before. "Fair enough," she said with a nod. She could handle his playful side as long as it didn't get in the way of having a baby.

"Good. I'm glad we got that settled. Now, let me ask you what our chances would be if we did it right here, right now, on this desk?"

Her jaw dropped as her gaze rocketed to the uncovered windows a mere fifty feet away. "I think the chances of us getting caught and ruining my business reputation would be excellent."

Her face must've been a jumble of horror because he started to laugh. "It was a joke."

"Of course," she said, taking advantage of his lighter grip on her waist to move further away from him.

"So laugh already." He stood and stepped toward her.

"Ha ha. How's that?"

"Shitty." He stepped toward her again.

His crooked grin worried her. "Whatever you're thinking, Tony, don't do it."

But he did. He wrapped both arms around her waist and walked her backward as he dug fingers into her sides, tickling her. It was so absurd. She hadn't been tickled since childhood. What else could she do but laugh, letting him win this strange battle for control of her mood? And he got the added bonus of her clinging to him for balance.

Trish reflexively shoved her face against his shoulder and breathed him in, all laundry soap and warm spice. Miraculously, her uptight tendencies scattered, and she reveled in the closeness… until the door chimed.

Tony froze, and Trish peaked around his body to see the wide-eyed tile rep.

"Am I early?" the well-dressed man asked.

Trish tripped over Tony's feet, scrambling to her desk. "No. Not at all. I was just…" What? *Oh my God.* She felt the heat melt the makeup off her face.

"I was just leaving." Tony walked to her and placed a kiss on her cheek. "We'll finish this tonight." And then he strolled past the man with a nod of his head and disappeared onto the crowded street.

• • •

Tony made it two blocks to where his bike was parked before a phone call stole his smile.

"What do you mean she's filling with fluid? Fluid from where?"

"It's called ascites, and it's from the tumors," Angie explained.

"More than one tumor?"

"I guess. I don't know. It's hard to get a straight answer. Everybody seems to be hearing something different. Makes me want to go to the next appointment."

"You should."

"Tell that to our aunts."

Tony roughed his face in his hands and released a growly breath. "So what's this mean?"

"Ma says Nonna's abdomen is being drained to make her more comfortable and her treatment plan might change. And…no trip. She can't go to Italy."

"Shit."

"Exactly. Tone, I looked on the internet, and this could mean the tumors are growing and spreading."

The sickness in Tony's gut grew and spread to his heart. "Double damn."

"I know. Do you think you can have the car seats finished this week? I want to show her, take her for a ride, take her mind off this crap for however long I can."

"Yeah. You bet. Consider it done."

"And Vin moved the concert up."

Everybody was kicking into gear, readying for the worst. Tony's eyes burned. "Ange, do you really think she's running out of time?"

"I hope not, Tone."

He hoped not too. But just in case, ready or not, he and Trish needed to speed things up.

After hearing pretty much the same thing about Nonna's condition from Ma, Tony swung by Angie's and worked until his fingers ached. When he left, the car was ready to roll.

Riding away from the garage with wind in his face, he questioned the extreme he was willing to go to in order to give his grandmother something special. A baby. But when he stopped by her apartment, and witnessed the weak smile she offered for a loaf of Mancini's bread, he was convinced he'd go to any extreme to give her bigger joy. Besides, Tony was used to gambling and living at the extremes. How was this plan of Trish's any different?

Trish. Thinking about the way she responded to his attempts to make her relax made him smile. At least their kid would have one conscientious parent who towed the line. And that was better than he always feared he'd do. *You've got Vegas wedding written all over you,* Vin used to say. Considering the women Tony usually dated, that was a scary thought. Waking up tied to the likes of Brandy the Bartender was bad enough. Having a kid with her was a million times worse.

He thought about it as he parked his bike and jogged the steps to his flat. Ultimately, he wasn't worried he'd end up married in Vegas, because after seeing the pain of his mother becoming a widow and Vin's ugly divorce, marriage lost its luster—not that it had much before. If you could get the goods without the gold, then why bother. And if you could get the kid, too? *Bing-to-the-O.*

Tony showered, shaved and thought some more. Nonna was dying. There was no question about that. Ma said ovarian cancer was tricky, sneaky, and symptom-free—until it was too late. There wasn't much they could do, but wait. For her to die. And that wasn't okay with Tony. Weddings and funerals, baptisms too. He had power here, power to give his family something to wait for besides Nonna's funeral.

He buttoned his shirt, zipped his jeans, and shoved into his boots. Stopping in the kitchen, he grabbed a six-pack of Heineken, 100 percent certain Trish DeVign didn't stock a fridge of beer. He wasn't nervous but after the pressurizing news about Nonna he wasn't feeling his usual carefree self either. Under the circumstances, he tried not to stress over it. He'd get to Trish's, have a drink, settle her down, and then they'd have some fun.

Thinking again about Nonna, he knew…there were worse ways to spend an evening.

By the time Tony made it to Trish's front door, he was ready. Having spent the last five blocks conjuring up images of her grinding in that grass-green dress and fishnet hose, he was halfway to a hard-on.

She opened the front door, eyes shiny and wide. "You came."

"Not yet." He smiled, unable to hold back the crass but teasing comment. She made it too easy for him to enjoy shocking her, making her blush. Somehow those little thrills wiped a lot of big worries away.

"I thought maybe you'd changed your mind." She clutched the doorknob in her left hand as she smoothed her right hand up and down her cotton-covered thigh. Black stretch pants clung to her legs with only the shirttails of an oversized oxford hiding the goods.

"I'm not changing my mind."

"Okay, then." She released a shaky exhale and stepped aside, waving him in. "But before we get started you should know that I don't actually ovulate for a few days. I read that sperm can live inside a woman for three to five days, so we should be good."

She was walking away from him, toward the stairs, but he heard the quiver in her voice.

He itched to crack open a beer. "Hey, wait."

She stopped on the first step and turned. "Yeah?"

"You're going to take advantage of me without even offering me a drink?" He lifted the corners of his mouth and the six-pack of beer.

"Tony, I read it's not good to drink alcohol when you're trying to conceive."

"You need to stop reading," he said with a chuckle. "Relax. Remember? Come on. One bottle won't hurt. Do you know how many babies were conceived because Mom and Dad got tipsy?"

She clutched the railing. "I don't want to get tipsy. I want to remember every detail. This is a big deal."

No pressure, Tony thought, rubbing his free hand on the back of his neck. Heck, he never felt pressure to perform when his performance was the focus. Here he was simply a cog in Trish's baby-making machine, and he was white-knuckling the six-pack. "Yeah, well, I need the beer. Consider it foreplay."

The corners of her eyes and lips drooped, and Tony had the distinct impression that he'd somehow insulted her without meaning to. "Fine. I'll get a glass." She bounded off the step and down the hall to her right.

"I don't need a glass."

"But I do," she called. "I'll meet you upstairs."

Okay. So much for the playfulness he managed to cultivate in her office today. Maybe after the beer.

He took the steps two by two, six-pack in hand, not knowing where he was going in a house this big. At the top of the landing, he saw one room with lights on. Walking there, he wrestled with weirdness. Angie would shit. Vin would shit. Heck, Ma would shit, too. But as much as he loved his family, there was no room for them in this bedroom—even though they were the reason he was here.

Standing in the doorway, he took it in. Opulent, feminine, floral, plaid, and gold. Decidedly Trish DeVign. He smiled, because she'd lit candles, dozens of them, despite her admission that she worried he wouldn't come. And there was music. He wondered if this seduction scene had always been part of her plan, too.

"Maybe I went a little overboard. Sorry." She pushed past him, pilsner glass in hand. "When I'm nervous I over plan. I mean, I'm a planner to begin with, but…" she waved her hand. "Never mind. Just give me a beer."

His smile widened, because, damn it, if she wasn't the most charming woman he'd ever met. He loved the way she flustered, but powered through. Setting the six-pack on a nearby table, he snatched two bottles, twisted the caps, and took the glass from her. As he poured the beer down the side of the glass and watched the golden liquid pool, the fun kicked in.

He stepped closer to her. "You know it's all in the head, right? So pay close attention to that. How it looks. How it feels on your tongue." He winked at her.

"Give me that," she spat, and taking the beer, she polished off half before he had his bottle to his lips.

"You know, I was talking about the beer."

"I know that," she said, wiping her mouth with the back of her hand. "But there's always a double meaning with you, isn't there?"

"What can I say? I enjoy myself." He set the bottle on the table beside him. "And you're going to enjoy yourself, too."

She drained the glass. "No pressure, Tony. I'm serious. Let's just make sure it counts." And with that, she turned, walked to the bed, dropped her glass on the bedside table, and crawled fully clothed beneath the covers.

He watched as she drew the comforter to her shoulders and shimmied beneath it. First the black stretch pants peaked out from beneath the blankets and dropped to the floor, followed by black panties.

"I'm ready," she proclaimed with a crisp nod.

Just like that. "You can't be serious."

She sat up, clutching the comforter to her chest, even though she wore a shirt. "I am."

"Why? Why would you want to do it like this? You have candles and music and…"

"You said downstairs that you needed a beer and the beer was foreplay. I get it, Tony. You're doing me a huge favor. Huge! And you're hoping to get something awesome for your family in return. This isn't about you being attracted to me. I can live with that."

But he couldn't, because nothing could've been further from the truth.

CHAPTER NINE

Trish wanted a baby, she didn't want to *be* a baby, and yet here she was with feelings hurt because Tony made a joke about beer being foreplay.

Come on. She didn't recognize herself lately, not since the night of her cousin's wedding when her usual poise under pressure crumbled in the face of Tony's flirting. What was the big deal? He was a nice-looking guy who was always up for some fun, and now he was going to help her get pregnant. She shouldn't be pouting because he wasn't *interested* in her. She didn't need him to be interested. This was a mission with one focus. Pregnancy.

He stood there, at the foot of the bed, beer in hand, and she wished beyond reason that she could send him away, go back to before, when he didn't know her deepest secret, when he didn't have her running scared.

"What makes you think I'm not attracted to you?" He walked to her, placing the beer on the bedside table.

"Honestly, Tony, I don't want to have this conversation. I don't."

He sat, narrowly missing her legs still stuffed beneath the covers. "But I do. And you know, making a baby together sort of entitles me to be heard."

"Then let's not do it." She shoved at the covers and wiggled off the opposite side of the bed, fully aware that her bottom half was bare beneath the oversized T while Tony sat guard over her leggings and underwear. "This was a mistake. We have too much in common, like work and Ange. I got caught up in the possibilities and clearly didn't think it through." She walked the perimeter of the bed, eyeing her pants.

Tony lifted a foot and dropped it slightly to the left, pinning her clothes beneath his boot. "Fine. We don't have to make a baby. But if you think for a minute I'm leaving here before I get something in return, you're crazy."

She stopped, narrowed her eyes, and punched hands to hips. "Is this another joke?"

"Maybe. Maybe not. Either way, I think you should lift up the shirt."

"Excuse me?" Pressure built inside her head, heating her face, and bugging her eyes.

"You've been teasing me for two weeks, ever since that birthday party and your comments about the cake."

"My comments? What comments?"

He flattened his palms against the mattress and leaned back, just a smidge, not enough to free her clothes, but enough for his leather jacket to fall open and his fabulous chest to strain against his shirt. "You know what you said, and you know why you said it."

She scoffed and wiggled a bit, hoping to shed the shivers from his stare. "I don't know what you're talking about. I was with Jackson that night."

"Uh huh." He smiled. "But you wanted to be with me."

Trish shut her mouth so hard her teeth chattered. Had she been that transparent? "Tony, stop it. Give me my pants and go."

"Okay. As soon as you lift the shirt and put me out of my misery."

She rolled her eyes. These games might work on his usual conquests, but she wasn't usual, and she wasn't his conquest. "Never mind. I do own other clothing, you know?" She turned her back on him and walked to her dresser.

Before she could open a drawer, his arm looped around her waist and he spun her to face him while crushing her body against his. "Let's get something straight." His mouth hovered inches from the tip of her nose. "Long before you hit me with this crazy plan there was something brewing between us."

The hint of beer on his breath, the strong arm locked across her back, the heat rising between them. She'd planned for a lot, but she could've never planned for this. She blinked, grasping for control of her wayward emotions. "So you admit this plan is crazy."

He grinned. "Don't change the subject." And then he lowered his cheek to hers, smoothing skin to skin until he was nibbling her ear, licking the lobe, drawing it into his mouth, leaving her breathless. "For the record, I am very attracted to you."

"You are?"

"I am." He backed her into the dresser, hooking a hand beneath her knee, and hiking her leg along rough denim.

Trish shivered. Something rough and unfiltered stirred in her chest, urging her to drive him back toward the bed and see this thing through.

"Despite what you may have heard, I'm a gentleman," he continued, adding his trademark grin. "And you asked me to leave. So I'm asking you, is that really what you want, or should I stay and finish this?"

Beneath a hypnosis caused by Tony's beautiful face—bold black brows, dark chocolate eyes—Trish wanted the baby, but suddenly somehow she wanted the man more. "Stay." It was a hurried answer made by her overheated body instead of her overused mind.

A second later, his lips met hers, shocking her body with pleasure and giving her mind a much-needed break. It was impossible to think straight while being electrocuted, so she didn't try. She surrendered to her tingling skin and racing heart, neither of which was necessary to get pregnant. But when his tongue invaded her mouth, making thought soupy and knees weak, she decided the chemistry was a welcomed bonus. At least she wouldn't have to grin and bear it, not while his fingers crawled along her bare thigh and his mouth dropped to her neck. She squeezed her eyes shut and blocked her nervous chatter, threading fingers through his soft, thick hair, holding his head as he sucked the skin on her throat. Her sigh echoed in the silence. Burying her nose in the blanket of black, she breathed him in and let him consume her.

Just as she managed to fully relax in his arms, he spun her away from the dresser, releasing her onto the bed. Her shirt wound around her waist, and she scrambled to cover. Instinct.

"Too late." Tony smiled. "I saw what I saw, and I liked it." His jacket hit the floor. "Your turn."

"For what?" She gulped to go along with the blush.

"I lost the jacket. You lose the shirt."

She glanced at her jumbled shirt. "No way. I'm pantless. You're not. We're hardly even."

"Fine." He unbuttoned his shirt, widening the V at his neck, and then lifted the fabric over his head, pitching it to the floor. "There. You're bottomless. I'm topless. Call me even."

She'd call him mouthwatering. Hard and rough. Dark and light. A breathtaking balance of masculine beauty. And then there were the tattoos, strategically peppering his arms and abdomen so she noticed his best places, like his bicep, where the Italian words she'd noticed before looped his muscle, and his forearm, where a large star and rambling vines marred his flawless skin.

But there were unexpected works of art as well, ones he kept hidden beneath T-shirts and faded Oxfords. She eyed the fiery comet covering the uppermost part of his right pec. A tail of orange, red, and blue sprawled over his shoulder and disappeared around his back. She lingered there, noticing how the muscled chord of his neck created a gentle swell at the juncture with his shoulder. Her lips twitched, wanting to taste it. She swallowed too hard, knowing she stared too long.

"When you're done admiring the goods, you can return the favor."

She choked down the embarrassment. "Nope. We're not even until you're pantless, too."

He chuckled. "Oh yeah? Well, ditto for your top."

She would've rolled her eyes had they not been busy ogling his chest. And her brain, it cried for sanity. She was slipping further and further away from the simple purity of her plan. Have sex. Make baby. There wasn't a single bullet note on watching each other undress. All they needed to do was the deed—missionary style—on the right days, and then wait for the positive test result.

But Tony changed the game, didn't he?

He flicked the button on his jeans and tugged down the zipper, revealing gray boxer briefs. "Come on. Gimme something."

"Fine." Which was a complete understatement. She wasn't fine. She was rolling onto her knees and reaching gingerly under her top to wiggle out of her bra in front of this gut-wrenchingly gorgeous man. *Fine?* She balked and pulled the bra out through her sleeve. "There."

He waggled his brows. "Tricky, but I can see your nipples."

She slapped her arms around her chest. "You shouldn't be teasing me now."

"No?" He walked to the bed until his legs touched the mattress. "Then tell me what I should be doing?"

She would if she could. The problem was, nothing she planned seemed to fit with this man and this moment, meaning she was improvising, something she avoided like horizontal stripes. Improvising led to foolish mistakes and a loss of control. Improvising led her here, to this bed, where a shirtless, grinning Tony Corcarelli loomed over her. For better or worse she'd seen the last of her simple, straightforward plan.

God help her with whatever happened now.

• • •

Tony figured Trish spent lots of time ironing out details, including how the deed would go down. He grinned, because knowing Trish, the all-business Boss Lady, "going down" wasn't one of those details. But after the kick in the crotch he got from kissing her, he had his own ideas about her little plan. And after the way she responded to him, he didn't think she'd mind the detour.

"Maybe you could just stop talking and get busy making a baby," she said, sitting on her knees in the middle of the bed, crisscrossing arms over breasts. If it weren't for the wide eyes and flushed face, he'd think she was disgusted by him. But he saw the way she gawked at his chest, and there was nothing disgusted about that.

"So that's how it's going to be," he said, dropping his pants and boxers to the floor with one push.

She zeroed in on the goods for a second. Her eyes growing even wider, but then she looked away, reaching behind her for the edge of the comforter. "Seriously, Tony, it'd probably be best if we didn't say anything else now. Let's just…"

He dropped to the bed, grabbed her and pulled her to him, knees to knees, chest to chest. Gathering the hem of her shirt in his hands, he tugged the soft fabric over the curves of her bottom and back, stroking soft skin as he went. His breathing quickened, matching hers. When she was naked, pressed against him, he stole a glance between them.

"There," he whispered. "Now we're even."

She didn't seem bothered by his talking now. She matched his crooked grin, a look he hadn't seen before, just the tilt of her lips, a sparkle in her eye, and he wanted her in the worst way.

He pressed against her until she toppled backward, sprawling on the mattress beneath him. And then he kissed her, hard and punishing, squeezing her face in his hands. She whimpered, grabbed hold of his wrists, digging nails into his flesh, and then she arched into him, trapping his erection between them, milking it with rolling hips.

Tony swallowed a growl. Making a baby would be damn near impossible if he gave in too soon. Raising onto his hands and knees, he straddled her, releasing some of the pressure to his groin. Another kiss. A brush of palm across her nipple. Her hands smoothing down his sides. The blood pounded through his veins, pooling in his penis.

Tony dipped his lips to her shoulder and then to her breast. As much as he wanted to linger, he needed to keep moving, to get away from her hands that were crawling across his lower stomach, inching toward the launch site. One touch, and he knew he'd be over.

He dropped his mouth to her stomach, licking her skin. His hands roamed, grazing her thighs inside and out until his fingers opened her. She was wet enough to finish this, no need to delay, but the faint floral fragrance of her skin on his lips urged him to taste the rest.

Shoving his hands beneath her, he lifted only to feel her muscles harden in his hands.

"Tony, don't. You don't have to. It's not necessary."

His gaze grazed the center of her body, past her taut belly button, between her swollen breasts, to find her staring down at him, brows furrowed even as her chest heaved. "But I want to," he said. And when he did, she unclenched her butt cheeks, dropped her head to the pillow and moaned.

Apparently he'd found the ultimate way to relax Trish DeVign. He smiled as he kissed, licked, and teased.

She moaned again, squirmed, yanked his hair, and then she lifted her body to him, pressing against his mouth. More tortured noises. More hair pulling. He was hard as a rock, avoiding contact with everything and anything, praying for not so much as a brush of air. And then she broke. Shattered. Muscles shaking. Breathing in sobs. He crawled over her to find her eyes closed and her arm flung over her forehead.

"That was not part of my plan," she whispered.

"I figured, but I like my plan better." He kissed her, wanting for her to taste the proof of a good plan on his lips.

Several seconds passed before she returned the enthusiasm of his kiss, but when she did, there was no mistaking the boost of energy. She drilled his mouth with her tongue as she reached between his legs. This time, he didn't panic. He held his breath and rocked against her hand, hardening every inch of his skin, feeding the ache to a fraction of the edge, and then he cranked her knees higher, lifting her hips. On a single, labored breath, he drove inside.

Trish yelped at the abrupt movement, but before he could pull back and slow down, she gripped his neck and yanked his face to hers. "You were right," she managed between heavy breathing. "I did want to be with you." And then she kissed him, driving her tongue into his mouth again, matching the rhythm of their lower halves. She clawed at his shoulders, nibbled his lip and drove him crazy, until the edge was a welcomed relief.

He collapsed on top of her with only sweat and breathing between them. Holy hell. That was…

"Do you think it worked?"

Was it wrong to wish against her, to hope it didn't work? Maybe it was lousy of him, but it was also true. Tony hoped he failed. He hoped Trish wasn't pregnant.

Because then they could do it again.

CHAPTER TEN

Trish rested her chin on Tony's shoulder and watched candlelight flicker on her ceiling. God, she hoped this worked, because if it didn't, they were going to have to do it again, and that was... She closed her eyes, tried to breathe, but his weight restricted the motion. What little air she managed to inhale was tinged with him, cedar and soap. She was entirely too comfortable in this position, and that wouldn't do.

Tony was simply a means to an end. No matter how attractive or good in bed, he wasn't a romantic possibility. He was a sort-of employee, her best friend's brother, and a man fundamentally opposed to settling down. She sighed, wanting her body to agree with her brain, to declare more sex with Tony out of the question, but who was she kidding? She'd never been closer to having a baby. But she'd also never been closer with chaos. And why? Because Tony made the loss of control exhilarating.

"We should do it again, just to make sure," he said, nuzzling his nose against her neck, blanketing her skin in shivers.

"Tony..."

The doorbell rang followed by three loud knocks that ricocheted through her exhausted body, rattling her cells to attention.

Tony lifted, hovering above her on the palms of his hands. "Were you expecting someone?"

"No." Trish scrambled out from underneath him, snatching her pants from the floor. "But what if it's Ange? Your bike's parked in front. She'll..."

The warm, wet sensation between her legs startled Trish. She'd never had unprotected sex before. And although she knew what they'd done and why they'd done it, the proof of their action slightly overwhelmed. With a giant inhale and a squeeze of her muscles, she clenched her thighs, hoping to lock the fluid in a few seconds more, not wanting to lessen her chances of conceiving. But the doorbell rang again, and then her phone. Trish blinked her brain to attention, wiggled into her pants and glanced at her nightstand where the phone sat next to Tony's discarded beer. *Mom.* She snatched up her phone and then her shirt from the foot of the bed and glared at Tony. "Stay put," she warned. "It's my mother. I'll get rid of her."

Trish bounded down the stairs, heart in her throat. She had no idea why her mother would stop by unannounced at—she looked at the grandfather clock—ten o'clock. She hoped it wasn't an emergency.

Smoothing her hair with one hand and wiping a finger under her eyes with the other, she hoped to God she didn't smell like sex. Her mother was going to hug her and then ask a million questions Trish wouldn't know how to answer. Raising her shirt to her nose, Trish sniffed. Faint traces of Tony lingered enough to make her stomach wobble, but she opened the door anyway if only to foil the incessant knocking.

"I see Tony's here." Angie stood on Trish's front porch, lips in a grim line, envelope in hand.

Trish opened her mouth, looked at her ringing phone, closed her mouth, and then opened it again. "You're not my mother."

"Don't be a smart ass." Angie pushed Trish aside. "Where is he? I'll happily crash your little nightcap before it goes too far."

"He's, ah, in the bathroom."

Angie raised a brow and then gave Trish the once-over. "He didn't even take you to dinner, did he? If he took you out, you'd be dressed up. What is this?" She waved a hand up and down Trish's disheveled clothing. "Was it a booty call?" She shoved a finger to Trish's chest. "I may not be your mother, but I'm still worried, especially since…"

"Hey." Tony stood shirtless in jeans at the top of the stairs.

"Jesus," Angie spit, whipping her head from Trish to Tony. "You don't waste time, do you?"

Trish laid a hand on Angie's forearm. "You said you didn't care. You said you didn't want to know."

"Yeah, well that was before I realized he was going to take you to bed before he even took you to dinner."

"Ange, chill. What's the big deal? We're consenting adults."

"Shut the fuck up, Tony." She took a step toward him, like she might charge the stairs. "As far as I'm concerned, only one of you is an adult, and it's not you."

"Here we go again." Tony descended slowly, shaking his head. "How long are you going to hold it against me? How long? I didn't want to run the company. So what? Nobody said you had to do it."

"Because they knew I would do it. Because they knew I wouldn't back out. I couldn't back out after you already did. I was all that was left."

All Trish could imagine was a colossal confrontation in her foyer that would lead to a family feud. "Tony, go back upstairs."

His eyes widened, and his lips sort of sneered. "No. Not until you're ready to come with me."

Angie groaned. "Never mind. I'm going, because this is making me sick. I swear to God I'll puke if I have to witness another minute of your mutual disease, so here." She handed the envelope to Trish. "You forgot to sign it."

Trish recognized the business envelope, featuring her company logo in the corner. With unsteady hands she pulled a check from the envelope. Sure enough, the usual loopy endorsement was missing.

"I can't pay my crew until I can cash this check."

Trish squeezed her eyes shut on a wave of remorse and then opened them on a promise to regain her focus. "I'm so sorry. I must've been…busy." Preoccupied with Tony and the baby-making scheme was more like it.

Rushing to the catchall drawer in the bureau beneath the hall mirror, Trish rummaged among hair ties, paper clips, loose change, and keys until she found a ballpoint pen. "Here." She signed the check, drew a deep breath and faced Angie, who was glaring at a silent Tony. "I'm sorry. I really am." About all of it, because standing between Tony and Angie was never a place she wanted to be.

Angie snatched the check. "Thanks." She glanced up the stairs at her brother and then again at Trish. "I'd say enjoy the rest of your evening, but I don't want to make myself sick." She turned, took two steps toward the door, and then stopped. "Finishing Collins's hardwoods at eight, right?"

Trish couldn't think of what to do now, let alone what came tomorrow morning, but it sounded reasonable, so she nodded. "Yep."

"See you then." And with that, Angie stormed out.

So much for Trish's simple, uncomplicated plan.

• • •

Tony watched Trish, staring at the stained glass window, hand on the doorknob. She didn't move a muscle, but he knew the wheels in her head were churning at breakneck speed.

"Don't let her bother you," he said, walking to her side, placing his hands on her shoulders.

She moved her head from side to side as he rubbed away the tension. "How can I do that? She's my best friend. When she's bothered, I'm bothered." She dropped her chin to her chest.

He wrapped her up and drew her against him. "She'll get over it."

"But what if she doesn't?" Trish stepped away from him. "What if I've ruined everything? What if she never looks at me the same?

What if she never looks at *you* the same either?" When she looked at him, tears shimmered in her eyes.

"Ah, come on. This is Ange we're talking about. She's harsh, but she's decent. I've never seen her hold a grudge on anyone but me. You'll be good."

He chucked his knuckles beneath her chin and smiled, but inside he was furious with himself. Screwing around with Angie's best friend wasn't smart. Getting caught with Trish didn't do a damn thing but affirm his irresponsibility in Angie's eyes.

"You really think it'll be okay?" Trish sniffed.

"Yep. I do. She wasn't mad because we slept together, she was mad because I didn't take you to dinner first." He chuckled, because it was just like his non-traditional, carpenter of a sister to have traditional relationship views. "And you know what? She's right. That was pretty shitty of me. I brought beer and got laid. Typical one-track-minded male."

Trish matched his grin, but there was still worry in her eyes. "God, Tony, we really did it, didn't we?"

He wasn't sure which it she was referring to. Maybe she meant making Angie mad. But the way she pulled her bottom lip between her teeth and the tousle of her hair had him focused on another it. And *it* was explosive. And *it* was much more appealing than rehashing what had happened with Angie. "Yes, we did."

"Okay, so as far as Angie goes, I'll talk to her tomorrow, smooth things out some more. And as far as this goes..." she palmed her non-existent belly, "I wait until I miss my period to test. Of course, I could get a blood test sooner, but I'd like to keep this as normal as possible, because once I'm..." She interrupted her babbling with a slightly unhinged laugh. "Oh my God. Once I'm pregnant. By you. Tony." She turned to the door and then to him again. "If Angie was upset because you slept with me before taking me to dinner, can you imagine how she'd react if I got pregnant this soon?"

He blinked. Shit. He'd never thought of it that way. And Angie wasn't the only one with a reaction to worry about. Ma. Nonna. How did he expect to go from Trish's contract employee to the father of her baby without raising his traditional Italian-Catholic family's collective blood pressure?

"Your mother and Nonna." Trish slapped a hand over her mouth. "They'll think I'm a slut."

"*Puttana.*" He'd heard the word enough to know it.

"What?"

"That's what Nonna calls a whore. *Puttana.*"

Trish paled.

"Hey, hey, hey." Tony reached for her, but she backed away, pressing against the wall. "You're not a whore."

Her face wrinkled. "Thanks for that, but I hardly think they'd agree once they found out I was pregnant by you without so much as a dinner date between us." She banged her head off the woodwork. "What was I thinking? Angie was right."

Like fingernails down a chalkboard. Angie was always right, and it irked him. "Let's go." He marched up the stairs. "I'm taking you to dinner."

She scrambled after him. "Tony, it's not that simple."

"The hell it isn't. Ange knows we slept together. It's only a matter of time before she whines to Ma. But nobody can say a damn thing about it if we're dating."

"But we aren't dating."

"We are now." He grinned. "And don't forget to put on a bra. I can still see your nipples."

• • •

Sitting across from Tony Corcarelli in an IHOP restaurant, Trish surmised this was her life. There was some sort of poetic justice in it. Hadn't her mother always warned her about falling for the smooth-talking guy? Oh, and Tony was smooth. Otherwise, she wouldn't be caught dead inhaling a stack of chocolate-chip pancakes at midnight. She swiped at a dribble of maple syrup on her chin.

"Damn, you can eat." He smiled around a forkful of omelet.

"I eat when I'm worried."

"You talk a lot, too, which must make a big mess."

She chewed slower, wrinkled her nose in disgust, and glanced at her shirt to make sure it was syrup-free.

"I'm teasing," he said.

"You always are."

"Not always." He held her gaze with smoldering eyes.

Okay, she'd give him that. He could be serious when the situation warranted. There was nothing teasing about the way he made love. Not that they made love, she reminded herself. They had sex and hopefully made a baby. Big difference. Huge.

She took another bite of pancake and then dropped her hand to her belly beneath the table, rubbing back and forth. Was anything going on in there?

Angie's interruption and Tony's late-night dinner caused Trish to miss out on the obsessing she planned to be doing at home. She raised her other hand, wrapping it around a glass of orange juice. What were the chances she was pregnant on the first try?

Taking a sip, she held the cold liquid in her mouth until it warmed and then swallowed. She wanted to be pregnant on the first try, because prolonging interactions with Tony had become unnecessarily complicated. *But we aren't dating*, she'd said to him. *We are now*, was his reply. Why did that silly technicality make her tummy tumble? Dating Tony was a front, so his family didn't see her as a slut once the test turned positive. She needed to keep that in mind if she was going to get through the next nine or so months sane.

"So what's on the agenda tomorrow?" Tony sprawled in the booth, arm flung across the back, plate pushed away from the edge of the table.

Trish blinked. "What agenda?"

"What do you have planned?"

"Work," she said, leery of where this was going. He'd asked to do *it* again before Angie interrupted, and now they were "dating." Surely he didn't plan to exploit their interactions, and yet, this was Tony she was talking about.

"What kind of work?"

"Interior design."

He bobbed his brows and tilted his head. "Are you this difficult with all your dates?"

"Maybe." Hardly. Only him. He made her do the damnedest things.

"Then I can see why you're still single."

She tossed her napkin across the table at him. It flopped against his chest. He simply smiled and tossed it back.

"You're going to need that for cleanup, what with all the eating and babbling," he said.

She couldn't stop the smirk. "Fine," she said, dropping the napkin into her lap. "I'm working on the Collins's house tomorrow morning. Angie's laying hardwoods in the addition, and I'm meeting with cement contractors. Tomorrow afternoon I have blocked off for shopping. They're minimalists, so it's something different."

He nodded while he dipped a finger into a clump of whipped cream on the edge of her plate. "How does a frilly traditionalist shop for a minimalist?"

"Very carefully," she said with an easy smile. "Or else the minimalist ends up with a floral-patterned, oversized ottoman where a recycled-materials coffee table should be."

Tony straightened, sucked the cream from his fingertip with a smack of his lips, and rested his elbows on the table. "Where'd you find a recycled-materials coffee table?"

"No place yet. That's what I want to buy, but I can't find what I'm looking for."

His brows inched higher on his forehead. "Then let me make it."

"I thought you only upholstered furniture."

"Honey, you've only scratched the surface of what I can do."

Her tight skin burned. Ever suggestive, always the flirt, he riled her insides until she squirmed on thoughts of the other things he could do. Put it this way, the man had a very talented tongue.

Trish nearly groaned in disgust at the way her brain and body were behaving. Yes, he was attractive, but she refused to pine over him or make him more important than he was. As warped as it sounded, all she really wanted was his baby. She needed to remember that.

Life was entirely too complicated already.

"I'll tell you what. I have a few sketches of what I'm looking for. You can take a look and see if it's something you'd be interested in, but no guarantees. If I'm not pleased with the workmanship, then I'm not buying." *There*, she thought. The easiest way to remember Tony's place was by putting him in his place. She was the boss.

His hands disappeared beneath the table, and he leaned forward until his chest was inches from his plate. "Sounds fair. And I'm not worried." A warm hand landed atop her thigh. "You'll be buying… again and again and again." He winked as he pressed fingers into the flesh above her knee. "I'm good at everything I do."

Trish shuddered. *Let's just hope you're good at making babies.* If she had to endure much more of this, she was headed for major trouble.

CHAPTER ELEVEN

Trish wasn't hungry, but that couldn't absolve her of lunch with Mom. So she sat in her usual seat at the club, staring over her mother's shoulder out the window at the golf course.

Angie was on her mind.

Talking hadn't gone as planned. When Trish arrived at the Collins's, Angie busied herself with work. The few times she paused long enough for Trish to speak, Angie pretended like nothing was different. Pretending like nothing was different made it feel like everything was different, especially when Angie cited an evening with Nonna as her reason for not hanging out with Trish. Maybe it was the truth. Maybe it wasn't. But if things were normal between them, Angie would've asked Trish to go along.

Trish didn't want this strain. That's why she was rethinking her plan.

A sweater-vested man with a caddy half his size walked the green moor. They had the same wobbly gait. Were they father and son? Trish bit her cheek. Some people were meant to be biological parents. Some people weren't. If she fell into the latter category, then so be it. But then her stomach cramped, and her heart jumped, and Trish immediately wondered if it was the baby.

She slipped a hand to her belly. Every twinge was a reminder that one time was all it took. She had unprotected sex with Tony around the time of ovulation. Pregnancy wouldn't be a shocker. As much as she wanted to rethink this plan, she'd already put it into motion, leaving her no choice but to improvise for a few more weeks. Then she could take a test, and if the test was negative, she could put a healthy distance between her and Tony, hoping to make things right between her and Angie. If the test was positive…

She didn't know what that would do to their friendship. She only hoped all the Corcarellis would be happy, because she would be.

She rubbed the non-existent bump.

"Darling, get more sleep. You have bags under your eyes. Or change your eye cream. You're not getting any younger, you know." Trish's mother paused for a sip of chardonnay. "Which is why I think you should consider something." Another sip of wine built anticipation. "Mary Perrault's son is in town for a couple weeks."

Trish sharpened her focus from the green outside the window to her mother's painted face. "Stu is in town?"

"Yes, dear. And he asked if you were seeing anyone. He wants to call you." Her glistening pink lips curled. "Looks like you have unfinished business."

"We finished any and all business when he moved to Paris."

"He may be moving back, but don't tell him I told you. Your father said the Paris operation isn't as productive as Glenn had hoped. But never mind that. Wouldn't it be lovely, darling, for you and Stuart to reconcile after all these years?"

Lovely? Comical, really. Here she sat with her hand on her belly which may or may not contain a speck of Tony's child, and the only man she ever loved wanted to call her while he was in town for two weeks.

Stu. Trish huffed a breath and returned to staring out the window, gazing at a pure white sand trap. Stu had been perfect for her. He was handsome, warm, and ambitious with an adorable propensity for making lists. In fact, she owed their breakup to the wisdom found in such a list, one that outlined the positives and negatives of a transcontinental relationship. Over a bottle of Cabernet, they listed the good and the bad, and when the bad hung below the good, they called the relationship off. Just like that. How did one argue in the face of sound rationale? She missed that kind of straightforward thinking.

"Stu's back," Trish mumbled.

"Yes, dear. That's what I said."

But what would Trish say to him? *Why yes, Stu, I'd love to have dinner with you, maybe rekindle the flame. By the way, how do you feel about the possibility of raising another man's child? I might be pregnant.*

Trish coughed on stomach acid until she choked.

"Darling, drink something."

Trish had the urge to drain her mother's wine, but the maybe baby in her belly made her reach for water instead. After a long drink cooled her throat, she nodded. "Mother, there's a slight problem with Stu calling me."

Dolores wrinkled her brows and leaned in. "Do tell."

Trish winced. "I'm sort of seeing Tony Corcarelli."

Dolores's eyes widened and her lips curled. "You don't say."

Oh, Trish said it, whether she wanted to or not, because what choice did she have? As long as there was a chance she was carrying Tony's baby, she had to act the part.

• • •

Tony was avoiding Angie. It was easier that way.

He saw the fire in her eyes at Trish's house, and he knew her anger wouldn't die. He had that effect on her, ever since he turned down their father's offer to run the carpentry business, resulting in his father's insistence that Angie buy out Tony's half. Fifty-fifty split, the feeble man had said. And who would argue with a guy who was dying? Angie sure didn't. She accepted the offer to take the company reins, and she bought out Tony two weeks after their father died. Tony was stupid enough to think that was the end of it.

He stared at Trish's sketches sprawled on his kitchen counter until his vision blurred. It wasn't so much that he hated carpentry. It was more that he hated being tied down to one thing. No sense of responsibility, Angie called it. He shrugged. Maybe she was right about that, too. After all, look what he'd done. He tried to get her best friend pregnant. Where was the responsibility in that?

His vision cleared, and the longer he looked at the drawings, the more his mind whirled with ideas for Trish's table. Brainstorming was better than dwelling on his tanking relationship with his sister. It was also better than wondering if one time with Trish was enough. The way he'd dreamed about her last night, he knew the answer to that question. It wasn't. He'd do it again in a heartbeat, because there was something about the way the woman made love, rougher than he expected, like all that prim and proper professionalism was desperate for a break. Of course, what she was really desperate for was a baby. Was one time enough for that?

In a blink, his thoughts became convoluted again.

With a growl, Tony shoved the drawings across the countertop and watched them float to the floor. What if she was pregnant? He thought all he wanted was bragging rights to a wish-list topping gift for Nonna, but he'd also get a kid. His kid. His and Trish's kid. He looked around 400 square feet of apartment and couldn't find room for a crib. Unless he sold the pinball machine, downsized the flat screen…or moved.

The money from the buyout sat there like a thorn in his heart, because if he spent too much, he worried he'd somehow make things worse with Angie. She already assumed he'd blown the majority on loose women and tattoos. Yeah, he'd had a few of both, but not enough to drain the account.

Still, the idea of moving, of altering his life that dramatically frustrated him, and he pounded a fist against the countertop. His willingness to take a risk got him into a hell of a mess this time.

When the intercom buzzed, Tony thought to ignore it, but then curiosity got the better of him. With Ma helping Nonna, and Nonna preferring to stay home, daytime visitors were far and few between. And if it was Angie, which Tony doubted, he needed to grow up and face her.

"Yo," Tony called into the yellowed box beside the front door.

"Tone, it's me. Lemme up," Vin said.

Tony obliged, waiting with the door ajar for Vin to make the two-flight trek. When he saw the black of his head bob above the bannister, Tony smiled. "To what do I owe the pleasure?"

"Invites." Vin held out an envelope. "It's kinda late in the game to mail them, so I'm hand delivering."

"Invites to what?" Tony asked as he opened the envelope and removed the black cardstock.

"An Evening with the Italian Tenors. Nice, huh?" Vin gestured to the professionally printed invitation.

Tony stared at the silver lettering. "Cripes. A little fancy, don't you think?"

"The guys sing in tuxedos. I booked Hillman Center. What did you expect? Construction paper?"

"An email."

Vin rolled his eyes and flicked a finger at the invitation. "It's Tony and guest, but bring somebody classy. This is a big deal."

Tony took a turn at rolling his eyes. Vin thought everything he did was a big deal, which made it extra fun to mess with him. "Somebody classy, right, like Monica from Princess and the Pole. She wears sequins."

"She also wears Lucite stilettos. No."

"I was kidding."

"Yeah, well, I'm not. This is a classy night for a classy lady. Nonna deserves it."

Yes she did, and Vin didn't have to worry, because Tony wasn't bringing a date that would embarrass him. "I'll be bringing Trish DeVign."

Vin's eyes bugged. "Playing with fire, aren'tcha, man?"

"I don't want to hear it from you, Vin. Angie's already said her peace, and believe me, that's enough."

"So why are you pushing it?"

Tony shrugged. "I like her."

Which was true. He'd always liked Trish, but now there was even more to like about her, like the way she dug her fingernails into his neck, all needy and hard and...He shook off the wayward thoughts, and focused on the real reason he was doing this. *Puttana* wasn't a name he wanted associated with Trish.

"I still think you're digging your own grave."

"Maybe. Maybe not."

"We shall see. Just do me a favor and don't let the shit hit the fan during this concert. I want it drama free. Make sure Ange knows, too."

Oh, that would go over well. *Ange, Vin doesn't want you causing trouble with me and Trish at the concert.* He could almost hear her maniacal laughter.

Vin smacked Tony's arm and then jogged down the steps. When Tony heard the main door clang, he knew there was no reason to be standing in the hall, but hell, he couldn't move, couldn't face what came next. He needed to ask Trish to Vin's shindig, parade her around his family like she was his girl, in front of Angie and Vin, Nonna, and Ma.

What had he gotten himself into?

• • •

Trish stared at her figure in the full-length mirror, which was not a favorite pastime. When she looked too long, she saw all the things she didn't like about her body, all the things that separated her from her flawless, ballerina-built adopted mother, things like freckles splattering her chest, a higher-than-normal waistline, broad shoulders, and crooked breasts, with the right one smaller than the left. But she'd forgive the size difference if her breasts ever managed to feed a baby. That would be miraculous. Nursing a baby was the direct antithesis of surrendering a baby.

With an exhale that dropped her shoulders a smidge, Trish patted her stomach below her belly button. If she ovulated and Tony's sperm managed to survive the twenty-four hours of upheaval that followed, she was technically pregnant. She frowned, because it was still a long shot. She was too practical and realistic to think one time would work.

But there was a chance. And as long as there was a chance, she couldn't take any chances with Stu, who left a message two hours ago. She hated the thought of ignoring him, but she hated the thought of further complicating what was already complicated.

Trish shook her head and shuffled into her closet. She ruffled the clothes until she settled on a CMU sweatshirt and a pair of yoga pants. As a rule, there were no buttons or zippers after work hours, and that wasn't going to change because Tony was on his way with pizza.

He tried to get her to go out, but with all this chaos swirling around her, she only wanted to hide, which was better done alone, but for some reason Tony insisted. Maybe he was still nursing a guilty conscience from the confrontation with Angie. They were supposed to be dating after all, and this was what dating couples did. They ate pizza and watched episodes of *Gossip Girl* on DVD. Okay, that was her version of what dating couples did, but ultimately this was her plan, wasn't it?

The doorbell rang as she put finishing touches on her braided hair, securing it with a band and tossing the tail over her shoulder. She padded bare feet over the area rug in her bedroom and onto the hardwoods in the hall. With each step, her heart beat faster. She'd read enough about pregnancy to know blood volume increased. Was that the cause of her racing heart? At the bottom of the stairs, she saw Tony's silhouette through the stained glass, and her stomach tumbled. Could she be getting morning sickness this soon and this late in the day?

With a clammy hand, she gripped the knob and opened the door to find him smiling on her front porch, pizza box in hand. A grocery bag dangled from his other hand.

"Delivery," he said.

She smiled back. "Hey, you." And stepping aside, she waved him in.

He didn't move. He stood there with that goofy grin on his gorgeous face. "I like your hair."

She felt a ridiculous blush creep up her neck and fan across her face. Silly. "Thank you."

He moved then, brushing by her, angling the pizza box toward the living room. When he passed, she leaned a smidge closer and drew a lungful of his air, as if on some level she knew just the scent of him would banish the worry of the day. They were in this together after all. In a matter of weeks he'd become her sole confidante.

"Where do you want it, kitchen, living room, dining room?"

Bedroom. She shut the door harder than necessary. *Where the heck did that come from?*

"Family room," she said slowly and deliberately. "I'm all set up in there."

He faced her, raising a brow. "Right. No televisions allowed in formal living rooms, which is another reason why they're wasted space."

"Televisions are welcome in a formal setting as long as they're hidden. If you prefer to watch in the living room on my nineteen-inch screen, then we can certainly forego the sixty-incher." She walked by him with a smirk, grabbing the heavy bag from his hand.

He followed, chuckling behind her. "I'm good with sixty inches."

"I figured you would be." She looked inside the bag. A clear plastic container of the salad she requested rested alongside a two-liter of diet caffeine-free soda. This time, he didn't come bearing beer. She wasn't sure what to make of that.

On one hand, beer represented his need to calm both their nerves before they…Thinking about having sex with Tony while he was walking behind her did uncomfortable things to her skin. She fidgeted against the prickles. On the other hand, beer sort of signified the plan to relax and maybe take things too far. She fidgeted again. What did soda signify?

"Half pepp, half cheese, just how you like it." He put the box on the wet bar counter next to the paper plates and flipped open the lid. Drawing a deep breath over the pie, he hummed. "Mm, mm. There's nothing like pizza." And then he picked off a piece of pepperoni and tossed it into his mouth. There was something charming about the mannerless adoration. And that was Tony in a nutshell, charming despite the lack of refinement. He was good company, too.

She unloaded the bag, placing the soda on the counter near the sink, and dumping the salad into a nearby bowl. As she worked, Tony wandered over to the big screen, where he whistled.

"What are you a fan of that requires a TV this big? Wait…" he held up a hand, "don't tell me. Mixed martial arts?"

She wrinkled her nose.

"You're a gamer then, aren't you? Call of Duty? Halo?"

She nodded. "You caught me. I'm a regular sniper."

He picked up the DVD case which was resting on the end table. "No way. This is what you do? That's a slap in the beautiful face of this screen."

"That's what *we're* going to do. And it's good, mindless entertainment. You can handle it."

"Yeah, but why would I want to? The only reason a guy watches this crap is to get lucky with the girl who wants to watch it in the first place." He stared at her with a sparkle in his eyes and a hitch in his lip.

The deafening sound of an opening soda bottle filled the room. Trish had no idea what was coming over her, but flirtatious words she could never imagine saying pushed against her lips, demanding to be said until she couldn't hold them back any longer.

"So, are you going to watch it with me or what?"

She needed sunglasses to weather his full-blown smile. "Sure," he said, walking to the bar, grabbing a piece of pizza and taking a generous bite. "As long as we're clear on the motivation."

Oh, they were clear. He wanted sex. For fun. And the same mischievous part of her that spoke those flirty words couldn't be giddier. Of course, the sensible part of her would commence worry any minute now.

"If I watch that garbage, then you'll be my date to Vin's concert for Nonna." He nudged her with his elbow. "It'll be our first official appearance at a family function as a couple."

Let the worrying begin.

CHAPTER TWELVE

Trish had been to dozens of Corcarelli family functions over the years, but always as Angie's guest. Going with Tony was going to be weird. But if she was gutsy enough to make a baby with him, she better be gutsy enough to face his family while hanging on his arm. Nonna and Mrs. Corcarelli might find it strange. Vin might be hostile. She could handle that.

Mostly, Trish was worried about Angie.

"I'll deal with my sister," Tony said, like he could read her mind. But he couldn't, he probably saw her staring at the picture of Angie and her in Cabo last year.

Now Trish couldn't get Angie to follow her across town, let alone out of the country, and the distance between them weighed heavy in Trish's bones, making her tired enough to let Tony fight this battle with his sister. But that wasn't fair to him. Angie and Tony's relationship was already strained. He didn't need Trish and her cockamamie plan making things worse.

"Technically I got you into this mess, so I'll be the one to smooth things over with Ange," Trish said, hiding a yawn behind her hand. "I may not look like it now, but I'm a formidable negotiator."

He grinned. "Yeah, I know what you're capable of." His hand rested on the granite inches from hers, and she had the irrational hope he would touch her. Irrational because he'd touched her enough—this month anyway. Wanting him to touch her more was overindulgent and a one-way ticket to messy, considering the way he confused her plans and left her feeling chaotic. She stared at his tanned hand until her vision blurred, wishing messy wasn't also attractive.

"So, are we going to watch this thing or what?" Tony said, moving his hand away from Trish's.

She blinked and then saw him carrying a plate of pizza toward the couch. Disappointment reigned, but it was better than guilt or regret, two emotions that would be in high supply if she succumbed to basic desire while her friendship with Angie was floundering and Stu was back in town. *Stu.* She should've called him back and told him...what?

"Aren't you hungry?" Tony asked as he sat.

That was when she realized she was shuffling toward the couch with nothing but the two-liter of soda in hand. "Of course, I..." she lifted the bottle, "I was wondering if you wanted some."

He wrinkled his nose and shook his head. "Nah. That's for you. My cousin drank it while she was pregnant, so I figured it was safe in case...you know...you're pregnant, too." He shrugged and bit into his pizza, working the dough with a mouth that mesmerized her, from the perfectly pale lips to the dark dip in his cheek. "I also figured you had beer left from the other night, so I'll grab one of those."

He wanted a beer. After her earlier thoughts about beer being an antidote for nerves and a booster of vulgar behavior, she wondered if it was possible he only came tonight to eat and drink. She was thinking too much, wasn't she? It was just a beer, for God's sake.

Trish inhaled away her stupor and turned toward the kitchen.

"Hey. Ho. Sit. You don't have to wait on me. Power up your prissy show, and I'll be back." He sauntered past with a delicious smile and a piece of pizza in hand.

For a man who was nowhere near her perfect fit, he sure had moments when she wished he was.

An hour later, with the lights dim, and her legs crossed at the ankles as they rested on the cushion beside her, she realized Tony was the perfect fit for her oversized couch—a couch he'd upholstered a year ago, which he pointed out. Not that she needed the reminder. Ever since her cousin's wedding she was acutely aware of the pieces of Tony Corcarelli upholstery littering her house. It was like a part of him was always here.

She'd spent the last ten minutes watching him watch the television. A slow smile played on his face except when he was drinking his beer. She liked having more than his furniture around. She liked having him. His presence made the place homier. She wished she didn't feel that way, not about him. This house was made for a family, but Tony wasn't exactly a family man. He loved *his* family, but they seemed to be enough. She had no doubt he'd love a child if they managed to create one, but he'd made it clear he wasn't looking for a wife, which was fine because Trish wasn't necessarily looking for a husband, not right now, and not a husband like him.

Tony wrapped a warm hand around her bare ankle and squeezed, causing her to jump.

He chuckled. "Apparently you think this crap is boring too, because you're staring at me instead of the TV."

She looked at the screen, where nothing registered in her cloudy head. "I'm sorry. I'm…tired." She yawned liked she'd done throughout the evening, but this time was more for show.

He angled his body so he was facing her instead of the television, his hand remaining hot on her skin. "Could that be a sign?"

"A sign that I work and worry too much, yes. A sign that I'm pregnant, no."

"Oh." He nodded. "So you don't think it worked?"

At first, the furrow of his brow came as a surprise to Trish, but then she remembered his reason for being disappointed. Nonna. Not Trish. Not the baby. Not a family to fill this house.

"I just think it's too soon to know. Maybe it worked."

He nodded again, but the furrow didn't fade.

"How is Nonna?" Without her easy connection to Angie, information was limited.

"There's fluid." Tony squeezed her ankle again. "She's tired. Uncomfortable. It's not looking good."

"I'm sorry." Trish had said it too many times where Nonna was concerned. It had probably lost its impact by now, but she didn't know what else to say.

"Me too." He slid his hand to her calf, milking the muscle as he stared over the top of her head.

Minutes dragged, with Trish afraid to move. She looked at the television, hoping to settle her heart's erratic beat, but her head throbbed, her hip cramped, her chest strained. She wanted to open her mouth and deep breathe. She wanted to shift her weight off her aching hip. But she didn't want to distract him. Something in the heavy air told her what might help, what could happen next.

And then he lunged forward, grabbing the remote control. "I'm done with this."

Without the flickering of the TV, the room grew darker. Only the pendant lighting from the kitchen cast a soft glow.

Tony's hand shifted down her leg until once again he held tight to her ankle. "I think we should do it again."

"You do?"

"I do." He pulled her leg from beneath her, eradicating any chance of her heartbeat returning to normal.

He straightened her other leg, and Trish shifted so her weight distributed between her butt and mid-back, pressing into the pillows. He moved closer, slipping a hand along her outer thigh, and all she could think about was having sex on a sofa he'd upholstered. Talk about irony. Talk about lunacy. She was getting carried away when she already had more than she could handle. "But Tony, maybe once was..."

"Not enough." He was above her now, bracing his weight on his arms, which straddled her, gripping the back and arm of the couch. "Don't tell me it was enough. I know basic biology."

She released a shaky breath and inhaled spice and beer. The familiar scent she'd come to associate with him revved her libido. *Basic biology.* Right? Well, biologically speaking, having unprotected sex more often around the time of ovulation did increase one's chances of conceiving, and since that was what they were trying to do, it did made sense. He made sense.

But then his warm, soft lips brushed hers, and nothing made sense anymore.

• • •

Tony was probably going to regret this. He'd never been an emotional sex kind of man. Years ago, he made a pact with himself to never be with a woman when he was feeling particularly high or low for fear that he'd associate her with joy or comfort. That sort of neediness crippled a man. Just ask Vin. And yet, here was Tony, torn up inside, wanting Trish to take away his pain. That was why he was planting kisses down her neck, wasn't it? Then again, long before the conversation turned to Nonna he'd been thinking about doing this, touching Trish in all the ways he felt oddly entitled to do.

He wasn't entitled to anything. She wasn't his. So why did she feel made for him to hold?

"Tony," she whispered into the breathy quiet of the room. "Maybe we should go upstairs."

"Maybe," he answered with his lips against her throat. But then she slid her hands beneath his shirttails, and he decided they weren't going anywhere.

Capturing her mouth with his, he tasted her with his tongue. Sweet like soda. Hot like sex. And then her fingernails bit his back, causing him to groan and release more of his weight onto the cushion of her thighs.

She roamed his back in chaos, pawing and clawing and driving him deeper into her mouth. He wanted to touch her too, but the bulky sweatshirt stopped him, until on a grunt, he broke the kiss and pushed to his knees, whipping his shirt over his head. "Now you."

She planted her hands against his abdomen, every wiggle of her fingers making him harder. "Not this again."

He was already tugging the hem of her sweatshirt over her belly. "Not what again?"

"The striptease act. I hardly think it'll be worth it with the lights off." Her fingers teased his stomach until they reached the button on his pants.

"We'll see about that." He yanked the sweatshirt above her breasts and buried his face in her cleavage. She smelled like springtime, and tasted like the warmest, sweetest dessert. This time, he was going to…

"Doorbell," she hissed, sitting with enough force to launch him off her chest. "Shoot."

She scrambled to stand, leaving him sitting with his head in his hands, a hard-on in his pants, and the thought that the people she knew needed some manners.

"Oh God. I can't tell who that is," she said from her crouch in the kitchen.

"Leave it," Tony growled in frustration.

"I can't. What if it's important?" She ran her fingers through her rumpled hair and sighed. "Why does this always happen to us?"

"Because your friends and family are rude. They should call first."

The doorbell rang again, followed by a knock. "I'm going to answer it. Put your shirt on." And she disappeared.

Tony leaned his back against the couch and mouthed an expletive into the darkness. There was a message in this, wasn't there? Ma would say God was trying to tell him something, but damned if Tony could ever figure that sort of thing out. Maybe God didn't want him messing with Trish any more than Angie wanted him to. Why did Tony find it so hard to do what other people wanted him to do?

A deep voice ripped through his wonderings. He couldn't make out the words, but he was sure they were being said by a man. Standing, Tony crept into the kitchen and crouched beside the refrigerator, holding his breath for the best chance at sound.

"I'm sorry. It was impulsive. I shouldn't have come. You're obviously ill…or something," the man said.

"No, I…Stu, I'm sorry I didn't call you back. I was…"

"Sick. I can see that," the man said. "Why don't you head back to bed and I'll call you in the morning."

Despite the dread rolling in his stomach at the overly familiar words, Tony nearly laughed. The guy was a douche bag. Trish wasn't sick, but Tony would happily take her back to bed.

"Maybe I can bring you some chicken soup and a bottle of pinot noir. How does that sound?" the man asked.

How did it sound? Awful, Tony thought, and then the dread in his gut ripped through his chest cavity like the bottle rocket he and Vin once put in Angie's birthday piñata. A teenage Tony lost privileges for a whole month because of that.

He wasn't coming out the loser tonight.

Tony stepped into the center hall before Trish answered the man. "Hey, babe. Everything okay?"

She spun like a demonic top, eyes wide, face red, hair escaping its band, and then her jaw dropped, probably when she saw Tony hadn't put on his shirt like she'd asked. He would've felt bad for shocking her if he wasn't blazing non-verbal threats from the center of his eyes at the stuffed suit on her porch.

"Oh, I see," said The Suit with a side part in his hair.

116

"Stu, I..." she turned to The Suit and then back to Tony again. "Can you give me a minute?"

Tony nodded, never taking his eyes off The Suit, never taking one step outside of the hall.

"Not necessary," The Suit said, shuffling backward off the porch. "It was good seeing you again. Hope you feel better soon. Tell your mother I said hello. Enjoy your evening. Again, my apologies."

There was nothing worse than a grown man babbling.

When Trish called out a good-bye and shut the door, Tony meant to relax, mission accomplished and all that, but then she turned on him with the same shock from before.

"What was that?" she cried. "What were you doing?"

"Helping you." Okay, now he wasn't so sure, but it seemed like a good idea five minutes ago. "That guy's a jerk."

"You don't even know him," she yelled.

Tony flinched at the hurt in her voice. Obviously, The Suit was someone important. Tony didn't like the feel of that. "I know all I need to know about him from that conversation. Ill? He thought you were sick?"

"Because I'm a mess." She pulled her sweatshirt away from her body, and then plowed hands through her unraveled hair. Strands kinked in spots where braids had been.

"Oh yeah? Well, I think you're beautiful, no matter what you're wearing." He grinned. "Although I prefer you naked, which you would be right now if that moron hadn't barged in. But you know what? I'm glad he stopped by, because now maybe he'll go out into your world and let everyone know we're busy, and they shouldn't stop by without calling us first."

She gasped and backed against the door. For a moment he thought her legs were going to give out, so he walked to her. "What? What'd I say?"

"Don't," she said, lifting her palms, signaling for him to stop before he reached her.

"Why?"

"You're making this too complicated."

"Is that what I'm doing?"

"Yes. It's always what you're doing." She clenched her fists. "There is no *us*, Tony. *We* can't be beyond what we hoped to accomplish by having a baby."

"Why? Because of him?"

She froze, mouth as wide as her eyes. Tony didn't know where he was going with this line of questioning, and he didn't know why he wanted to go there. He didn't want *we* and *us* anymore than she did. This was about a baby. No more. No less.

"You should go," she said, stepping aside from the door.

"I should." But he didn't. He stood there, staring at her flushed face, wishing to God he could say or do something to make this right. And in a few silent seconds, he knew there was nothing he could do.

Stuffed suit, side part, proper talker Stu—Tony nearly choked as the name flashed in his brain—that guy was right for Trish's world. Tony was wrong. Oh sure, he was good enough to make her baby, but he wasn't good enough to be her man. Not that he wanted the job.

"Why aren't you going?" She stared back at him, arms folded across her chest, like she was trying to cover her heart or wished he would cover his.

"I need my shirt."

"Then get it."

He nodded and made his way through the house to the family room, littered with pieces of their evening. Pizza box. Beer bottles. DVD case. His shirt. Why did this suck like a breakup? They were never together to be pulled apart. He was acting like a girl. So what if he didn't get laid? Big deal. There were more mermaids in the sea.

"I'll call you."

He grabbed his shirt off the floor, and then turned to see her standing in the kitchen. Soft light from a nearby pendant sparkled in her copper hair. She was wringing her hands and looking so lost, he wanted nothing more than to hold her until they forgot every unpleasant thing.

"I'll call you about the table and Nonna's concert," she continued. "If…you still want to do those things."

What was he supposed to say? He nodded, shrugged into his shirt and pushed past her despite the urge to draw her near. Holding her wouldn't change anything. In fact, it would probably only make one thing clear.

Tony wanted more than a baby with Trish, but that was out of the question.

CHAPTER THIRTEEN

Tony glanced around Nonna's dining table at the somber faces sucking pasta into less-than-talkative mouths. Sunday dinner didn't feel like Sunday dinner anymore, what with Nonna wasting away at the end of the table and Angie barely talking to him.

Today was the day of the car presentation, and Angie didn't even ask him to wipe down the leather. No biggie, he thought as he sucked a piece of spaghetti into his own quiet mouth. Nonna didn't notice his workmanship. There was no way she could've seen a detail through all those bittersweet tears.

While Ma and Aunt Connie took Nonna to lie down, Tony helped his other aunts clear off the table. He was looking forward to their chatter about shopping and thick-headed men, but it never came. They talked about Nonna getting sicker, and Tony couldn't wait to get away. The minute the last dirty plate hit the laminate counter, he set out in search of Vin.

It figured Vin was with Angie, standing alongside Nonna's Cadillac.

"What's going on in there?" Vin asked, while Angie turned her back to Tony and polished the fender with her sleeve.

Tony swallowed his ever-present discomfort. "The same."

"Moping."

Tony nodded.

"And that's why we're out here," Vin said.

Angie lifted her head. "I'm going to check on Ma." Like a typical woman, she left the men tossing in the wake of her moodiness.

"She's upset. Emotional day," Vin soothed.

Vin was six-feet, five-inches of former Marine. He didn't soothe. At least he didn't soothe well.

"She's pissed at me," Tony said. "Because of Trish, but now Trish is pissed at me too, so hey-ho..." he shrugged and slipped his hands into his jean pockets, "you know how it is."

Tony tried, he really tried to pull off nonchalant, but something in the way Vin raised his brows told Tony he failed. Hard.

"Why don't you tell me how it is?"

"Because I'm not your mom," Tony scoffed. "I don't go around crying about my business to anyone who will listen."

"Ooh. Not fair. Not fair." Vin sucked on his bottom lip. "You know the only reason a man rags on a defenseless woman, one who is right now nursing her ailing mother, is because he's too chicken to face the truth."

Tony's forehead tightened. "I'm serious. Shut up, Vin."

"Make me," he said with a grin, repeating the childish phrase that had become a habit where Tony was concerned. There wasn't a comeback.

Even if Tony could take the beast of a man, he wouldn't dare. Family. Forever. "Can we just talk about the car or something?" he asked.

Vin nodded, and for a second Tony thought he was free and clear.

"You fucked things up with Trish, didn't you?" Vin leaned against Angie's precious car, but then thought better of it and straightened, bringing thick arms across his mammoth chest. "This is where I get to say I told you so."

Tony lifted his face to the afternoon sun and cringed. Yeah, he fucked things up with Trish, but not in the way Vin insinuated.

Vin, Angie, everyone thought Tony wanted a slam-bam-thank-you-ma'am while Trish wanted a good old-fashioned relationship. Tony would die before he let them know the truth. Not just because it would make Trish a *puttana*, but because every last Corcarelli would read too much into what this meant for him. It didn't mean anything. He wasn't turning over some highly anticipated leaf. He didn't want to change. He was happy with his life. He just wanted Trish in it, and for that reason—along with the Nonna reason—he hoped Trish was pregnant. Then, like it or not, Stu or no Stu, Tony would be a permanent part of her life.

"Fine. I screwed up," he admitted with a steady gaze on Vin's face. "Happy now?"

Vin slapped Tony's shoulder. "Come on now. You know me better than that. I won't be happy until you're happy, man. Really happy, not this quasi bullshit you get by playing around."

Tony flinched, rolling his shoulders forward like he'd been socked in the gut. "Why do you even care?"

Vin shrugged. "Don't know. Maybe I miss the camaraderie of the Marines, all that living and working as one. Maybe that's how I look at us. A team." He wrinkled his wide nose. "Or maybe it's because you're the screw-up brother I always wished I had, the one I could beat into shape and then take all the credit for his success." He grinned. "Yeah, let's go with that."

He was trying to make Tony feel better, but by the rocks in Tony's gut, it wasn't working. Tony was such a tool. While he was out here moping about Trish, Nonna was in there fighting for her life, a thought that prompted a curse beneath his breath.

"What if you're wrong, Vin? What if there's no big success? What if this is it? What if Nonna dies, Angie hates me, and Trish ends up with Stu?" He choked—and not on the name.

"So there's more to this story?" Vin relaxed his posture, dropping his arms to his side and bringing his hands together at the waist, where he rubbed them together. "Let me tell you something about women. They need stability. If they think we're playing around on them or on life, they're not going to like it one bit. And a good woman will only take so much of that before she finds a man who can give her what she needs."

Stu. Tony clenched his hands into fists, but then he scoffed at Vin. What did he know about good women? "You're so full of shit, man. Who are you to be giving me advice?"

Vin nodded. "Fair enough. Go on, laugh and point out all the things I did wrong where Carrie was concerned, but none of that changes the fact I'm right about this. I've lived and learned. Now it's your turn, man. Your turn." He poked a finger into the skin over Tony's heart, emphasizing each word.

Damn. Now was one time Tony wished he could skip a turn.

• • •

Trish placed her elbows on her mother's dining table and dropped her face into her hands.

"I mean, multiple, giant tattoos. Darling, you had to know. You had to see them when…before you…" Her mother's sentence broke apart—thank God—amid sniffles.

Was she really crying over this? Yes, Tony walks around her house shirtless, and he has tattoos. Big deal. Trish looked at her distraught mother. Apparently it was a big deal to her…and Stu… and the entire Perrault family, who by now had certainly spread the news to every member of Three Rivers Country Club, which was Delores DeVign's greatest fear.

Trish, fortunately, didn't share the same societally conscious genes. "You can't measure the merit of a man by the number of his tattoos." Funny words, so funny she bit back a snicker. Tony would appreciate the wit, but her mother? Not so much.

Delores whimpered. "Oh no? Then tell me how you can measure his merit, because I thought I raised you better than that. He's a smooth talker, a pretty face. Oh, Trisha Anne. You let him touch you."

This time Trish laughed. She didn't attempt to hold it in. Her mother was going to need to double her current anxiety and anti-depression meds if Trish turned up pregnant.

"What about Stuart?" Dolores dabbed a white cloth napkin across her brow.

"What about him?" Trish said, sounding more casual than she felt. Ever since the showdown between Stu and Tony, her insides had been tangled like cheap embroidery thread.

"What do you mean, what about him? Are you really going to throw away another chance at him for a chance at this... hoodlum?"

Trish shook her head. Part of her problem was the unbelievable revelation that no romantic feelings remained for Stu. He'd stood on her doorstep, eager to see her, and all she could think was he looked older. She didn't want another chance at Stu. And as far as Tony being a hoodlum...

"Tony is a great guy, Mother. You know that. You thought he hung the moon the night of the wedding. In fact, you're partially to blame for this. 'Stay,'" Trish said, mocking her mother. "'One more dance, kids.'" Trish threw up her hands. "Didn't you see the way we were dancing? You had to know where that would lead."

Yes, Trish was tired of shouldering the blame for this crazy situation. It may have been her plan in the first place, but other people pushed her over the edge, pushy people like her mother and Tony.

Delores blushed and looked away from Trish, content to fiddle with the crystal salt and pepper shakers. "Yes, well, that was before I knew that he has tattoos."

What the heck, she might as well get it all out of the way...in case she was pregnant...in case her mother was going to have to love a baby that was half the product of a man with tattoos. "He rides a motorcycle, too," Trish said, bracing for the melodrama.

"Your father is going to..."

"What am I going to do?"

Trish inhaled long and loud before she looked at the willowy man, striding through the dining room. "Hi, Dad."

"Darling." He removed his golf hat before kissing the top of her head.

"Devlin, please, help me talk some sense into her."

Devlin smiled. "Trisha, stripes do not go with plaids. There. I talked some sense into you." He winked, like Tony loved to do.

Trish's heart hiccupped.

Dolores growled. "The man has tattoos! Mary Perrault says her housekeeper's son got hepatitis from tattoos." She shuddered. "Devlin!"

"Is he good to you?"

"I'm sure he's *good to her*. Did you see how he dances?"

"I meant, is he kind? Does he make you laugh? Does he help you? Of course, good dance moves don't hurt either."

If Trish could be biologically related to either one of her adopted parents, she would pick Devlin. In her own way, Trish loved Delores, but the woman was exhausting. She tried too hard, always wanting to fit in and be noticed. Devlin didn't worry about those things, probably because he worked too much and too hard to notice. He was who he was, like it or not. Serious confidence and swagger came from living like that. The man was charismatic, decent, and true…just like Tony.

Trish made the connection so swiftly and easily, her head lightened. "Is Tony good to me?" she asked, repeating her father's question, staring off into space. "Yes, he is. Very."

He was kind enough to bring her diet caffeine-free soda. When she was around him, she couldn't help but laugh. And he helped her. Big time. From work projects to this…She smoothed a palm below her belly button. Using her father's criterion of kindness, laughter, and helpfulness, Tony was far better to her than Stu had ever been. Plus, Tony thought she was beautiful in a sweatshirt with messy hair. Even her mother wouldn't go so far as to say that.

"Then I don't see any harm in it, Dolores. Tell Mary Perrault to mind her own business and go make me a sandwich for lunch."

Dolores gasped, but she regally rose from her chair and walked toward the kitchen.

"She only wants the best…for all of us. Try to remember that." Devlin kissed Trish on the head again and playfully swatted her arm with his golf hat. "Stay for lunch if you can."

Trish left five minutes later, after kissing her mother and assuring her for the thousandth time that tattoos were not a prediction of future prison time. She wasn't sure if she managed to allay all her mother's fears, but at the very least she propagated the charade should she be carrying Tony's baby. Better to have her mother think the baby was born from something real than to ever know the truth. And as an added bonus, Dolores wouldn't be heartbroken when the relationship didn't "work out."

Trish's heart pinched and her stomach clenched. She dropped a hand from the steering wheel to rub away the unrest. The relationship couldn't work out. Even if on some level she wanted it. Even if on that same level Tony wanted it, too. The idea that both of them were too comfortable in these romantic roles threw her for a loop as she stood in her foyer the other night, having just closed the door on Stu.

Yes, she and Tony shared a mutual attraction. Yes, he was good to her. Yes, he referred to them as *we* and *us* and acted awfully jealous when faced with Stu, but what were the chances they could make it work? What were the chances any couple could make any relationship work? Wasn't it something pitiful like fifty percent? With Angie and a potential baby between them, they couldn't take the risk. They didn't need bad blood. Break-up blood.

Nope, Trish thought, shaking her head. This was better, a little awkward, a little depressing, a little frustrating too, but certainly far from the misery she'd expect if they tried to be a couple and failed. At least she could pick up the phone and call him without worrying about the call disintegrating into name calling and general post-breakup venom. As if to prove it, she hit a button on her steering wheel and dialed up Tony.

He didn't answer.

What should she make of that?

•••

Tony looked at Angie striding toward him across Nonna's narrow backyard, and then at the ringing phone in his hand. *Boss Lady* glowed on the screen. Talk about being between a rock and a hard place.

He sent the call to voicemail and lifted his butt off the picnic table bench so he could return the phone to his pocket.

"Ange." He nodded.

"Tone." She nodded back, and then she sat beside him with a huff. She hadn't been this close to him on purpose in weeks. "This is stupid. I'm in there watching Ma and Aunt Connie help Nonna into the bathroom, and I'm pissed more at myself than I am at you for the distance between us. So can we quit being mad?"

"I'm not mad," he said, leaning forward, elbows to widespread knees.

"Okay, then can I quit being mad?"

Angie's version of an apology was more humorous than heartfelt. He glanced at her over his shoulder, and sure enough, she was squirming against the wooden bench and blinking uncomfortably into the sun.

"Yeah, you can quit being mad." He spied a clover in the grass and stretched to reach it.

"Good." She released a noisy exhale. "You can come back to work in the garage now. You're paying rent for the space, you know?"

"I know." He popped the head of the pinkish flower from its thin, green stem and tossed both pieces to the ground.

"No work?"

"I got work." A recycled materials coffee table, as a matter of fact.

"Then get it done," she said, rolling her right shoulder into his upper back.

Tony nodded, letting silence settle between them. Eventually birds on the power line squeaked. Tony was oddly thankful for the sound. It gave him something to focus on beside the things that remained unsaid, like Angie not mentioning Trish. He should be the one to ask if this truce extended to her, but after his conversation with Vin, Tony was all Trish-ed out. He didn't want to think any more about helping her, about wanting her, about why she didn't want *him*.

"How's Trish?"

It figured. Tony straightened until his mid-back pressed against the weathered table. He dropped his elbows to the scratchy wood and lifted his chin to the blue sky. "You should know how she is. You're her best friend."

"Don't be an ass, Tony. You've seen her more than me lately."

"Whose fault is that?" Maybe it wasn't nice and all, after Angie came out to make things right, but still…he didn't like the idea of Angie being rude to Trish.

Angie leaned forward and assumed Tony's former position, elbows to knees. She glared at him over her shoulder, her hard-set face framed by pitch-black hair. Her eyes were the most ominous black sometimes. "What do you want me to do, bleed? I said I'm sorry."

Tony chuckled. "No you didn't. You asked if you could quit being mad. That's not the same thing."

"Fine, then. I'm sorry."

She wasn't looking at him, so he didn't know if she was sincere, but those words coming out of her mouth were an oddity, so he decided to give her the benefit of the doubt.

"You owe the apology to Trish."

"Probably."

More silence. Tony thought about getting up and going inside, saying his goodbyes, but he dreaded every goodbye since Nonna's diagnosis. Each one felt like it could be their last, the way she pinched his cheeks and stared hard into his eyes. Intense. So he avoided goodbyes, prolonged them, anyway he could.

"Who's Stu?" The question spit from his lips like skunked beer, and immediately he felt like a moron. Avoiding goodbye wasn't worth acting like this.

"Never mind," he said, standing.

"She told you about Stu?"

He stopped mid-step and faced Angie. As much as the conversation made him uncomfortable, some part of him wanted to know. "I met the guy. Didn't like him."

"He's back? Holy shit."

"Back from where?" With a suit like that and a side-part to boot, it sure as hell wasn't prison, unless he was a white collar criminal. Tony could dream.

"He moved to Paris to front his father's European operations. A couple years ago, I think. Maybe three. Where'd you meet him?"

"At her house. He stopped by while I was there." Tony couldn't keep the sneer from his lips.

"Shit," Angie said again, her eyes widening.

"You don't say." Tony dropped his head and shoulders, and spied the decapitated clover littering the grass at his feet. What the hell was he doing? This was supposed to be about giving Nonna the ultimate joy. How had it turned into Tony being…?

"Wait a minute, are you jealous? Worried? You are. Both." Angie stood. "You think she's getting back with Stu? Did she tell you she was getting back with Stu? I thought things were good between you guys."

Too many questions. They mixed with the questions already crowding his mind. "Yeah, sorry. I'm done, Ange. No more. I gotta get outta here. Go for a long ride. I'm gonna clear my head. See you tomorrow."

He didn't wait for her protests. He trampled grass beneath his feet until he reached the backdoor. With a deep breath, he opened the screen and stepped inside, ready to face another goodbye, hoping this one wouldn't be the last.

But the way things were going, it'd be just his luck.

CHAPTER FOURTEEN

Trish guided her Volvo around the pothole at the top of her street and glanced in the rearview mirror at the original Andy Warhol painting secured in brown paper and bubble wrap, and wedged into the back of the SUV. Satisfied the painting was no worse for the trip from the framing gallery, Trish returned her gaze to the road and then to her house, looming ahead.

Angie sat on the front porch steps.

Trish blinked. Seeing her there was a dream come true…but why was she there, out of the blue, looking more somber than usual? Trish whimpered. What if something happened to Nonna? Or what if Angie and Tony had a blow out? What if Angie knew the truth?

This time when Trish tried to whimper, the breath caught in her throat. She'd never shared details of her baby plan with Angie, but they talked enough for Angie to know how much Trish wanted kids. Maybe in the midst of fighting with Tony, Angie mentioned Trish's desire for a family, and maybe Tony spilled the truth. Trish exhaled, because honestly, how could things get any worse? If Angie knew, then maybe they could figure out a way to go back to being best friends instead of distant co-workers.

Trish pulled alongside the retaining wall and into the narrow driveway, tossing Angie a nervous smile.

Angie stood, brushed the seat of her pants and offered a nod as Trish existed the car. "Hey."

"Hey," Trish returned, strangling her handbag. "How arc you?"

She huffed, and then sat again. "Shitty. So let's get this out of the way. I'm sorry." She sat there all stiff, staring at the callused palms of her hands. "I was worried about you. It probably didn't seem that way, but it's true." She smacked her hands against her thighs and wiggled, like she was trying to rid herself of the emotion. "Are we okay?"

Relief washed over Trish, slipping from the corner of her eyes and onto her cheeks. She dabbed at the tears with her fingertips as she walked to the porch and took a seat beside Angie. "We're good."

"Good. Now, are you okay?" She frowned as if she already knew the answer. "Tony, um…he told me about Stu."

Trish's stomach rolled on the realization that Tony and Angie had been discussing her. Funny, though. She wasn't bothered by the reminder of Stu. Thoughts of him sort of came and went without any visceral reaction. "You know, I don't feel anything for him. Something has changed. With him. With me. With both of us. I knew the moment I opened the door and saw him standing there. I'm over him."

"Because of Tony." Angie sighed and leaned so far forward her head was almost between her knees. "Am I right?"

After the conversation with her father left Trish thinking about all the ways Tony was "good to her," she hated to think about Angie's question, and she sure as heck didn't want to answer, so she stared straight ahead at cars rolling down the tree-lined street.

How would she answer anyway? If she admitted her lack of feelings for Stu was in any part related to Tony, which part was to blame? The plan for a baby, which complicated reconciliation with Stu, or her troubling feelings for Tony, which twisted her plan and her heart? Neither one was something she wanted to discuss with Angie this soon after mending what was broken between them.

"Do you love him?"

"Who?" Trish gasped, mortified at the thought of loving uptight, overwrought Stu again. But then she was equally horrified that the same quick thought about Tony didn't conjure similar objections. Certainly she didn't love him, couldn't love him. She was just coming to terms with being attracted to him and him being attracted to her.

"Do you love my brother?"

Trish rolled mashed lips between her teeth as her stomach pitched and her heart burned. "I...think I might be pregnant." It was a diversion, sure, but it was also true. She'd been feeling odd lately, hoping hormones were to blame, but she didn't know, and she was tired of obsessing by herself. If she couldn't share random emotions with her best friend, then where did that leave her?

"Shit," Angie whispered, but then her arm snaked Trish's shoulder and she squeezed. "I knew something careless like this would happen." She huffed. "Does he know?"

Trish nodded through a mix of relieved and guilty tears.

Angie squeezed Trish's shoulder again. "Well, what's done is done, and he knows what he has to do."

Trish opened her mouth to breath, not liking the ominous tone of Angie's voice. What did Tony have to do? Stand by Trish? Of course he would. But the way Angie clenched and released her fist as her hand dangled from the arm perched on her knee, Trish dreaded something more.

"It's all very preliminary," Trish said, hoping to soothe. "We haven't talked about details beyond the possibility that I might be..."

"He has to marry you. That's the honorable thing to do. And this time he'll shirk his responsibility over my dead body."

Maybe over Trish's, too, because this was way more than her heart and head could handle. Marry Tony? Her stomach pitched again. "It's not like that, Ange. Please, don't. I might not even be pregnant. There's still a week before I can test. But...if I am, you have to let Tony and me work this out...alone. I'm begging you." She reached up and squeezed Angie's hand.

Angie snatched her hand away and dropped her arm, returning to her rigid position, leaning forward so Trish couldn't see her face. "Don't beg. Dogs beg."

Ouch. The coldness in Angie's tone was worse than her words.

"Fine," Trish said, trying to sound assertive rather than overly emotional. "I'm *asking* you from the bottom of my heart. Let it be. Tony and I can work this out."

Angie's shoulders slumped, and her head fell forward further. Her breaths echoed in the evening stillness, leaving Trish to struggle for something to say.

But Angie beat her to it. "You know what I wouldn't give for a single day without worrying about the people I love?"

The knot in Trish's belly floated into her throat. This wasn't fair of Trish to put more strain on Angie and Tony's relationship, to give Angie one more thing to worry about when she was already worried out about Nonna. Trish patted circles over Angie's back. "I'm so sorry, hon."

Moments of raw emotion were far and few between them, even as best friends. Angie was stoic as a rule. This…this killed Trish, and she leaned her head into Angie's shoulder, not knowing what else to do. They sat like that for several minutes, absorbing the misery of the day.

"Ah, screw it," Angie finally said, straightening and sniffing like she wanted to vacuum up and seal away the emotional mess. "Just, ya know, be careful. And remember…I'm here if you need me."

A small smile tilted Trish's lips. "I always need you. And if things get complicated and I need you to take charge, I'll tell you. I promise."

Angie eyed her suspiciously, but then propped her elbow on her knee and lifted her hand, pinky finger crooked and extended. "You swear?"

Trish's smile broadened, and her laugh wrapped in sniffles from lingering tears. "I swear," she said, locking her pinkie finger with Angie's.

And just like that Trish's world was right again. Except for the part that included Tony. That part was going to take a bit more time to settle. Whether she was pregnant or not, she was going to have to face the fact that this plan was more complicated than she ever imagined, starting with her feelings for him and the feelings he seemed to have for her. Those feelings were going to be part of everything they did together from work to parenting—if she was carrying his child. Could they suppress those feelings, even if they didn't want to? And if they couldn't, what happened then?

She had the sinking feeling there was only one way to find out.

• • •

Shitty day, Tony thought as he opened a beer and settled on the couch. He'd been seeing Nonna's face in his tired brain since he left her house, trying to outrun Angie and all her questions about Trish. "You be good, Antonio," Nonna had said as she weakly pinched his cheeks. "Be happy." It was like a damn conspiracy between her and Vin, only Vin wanted Tony to become some alter-version of himself so he could *be happy* and win Trish. *Win Trish?* What kind of game was this? All he ever wanted was to make Nonna happy.

He leaned his head on the back of the sofa and balanced the bottle of beer on his thigh. After leaving Nonna's house, he rode miles with nothing but the wind in his face and pressure on his brain. He did a pretty good job of keeping coherent thoughts to a minimum, until he cut the engine and climbed these stairs, eager to be home.

But this didn't feel like home with its water-damaged plaster and flimsy single-pane windows, doing nothing to keep the cold wind and street noise out. Certainly it wasn't a home where he could bring a baby when it wasn't home enough for him.

Since when wasn't it home enough for him? He raised the bottle and chugged. *Since Trish* was the reply. Her house had him spoiled, what with all the master upholstery. He smiled, thinking of all the pieces he'd perfected for her, but then the expression faded. Lifting his head from the couch, he looked around the room, realizing not a piece of furniture was designed or modified by him. The uncomfortable couch he sat upon was a hand-me-down from Vin, a casualty of his doomed marriage. The piece was well-made and expensive, and Tony never felt the urge to make a change. From the bed to the dining table to a couple armchairs, the story was the same, all stuff given to him to take up space. Not a damn piece meant a damn thing.

If he could tell a lot about a person from their furniture, then what did his say about him?

He took a longer drink, draining the bottle on a single breath. How was it possible Trish owned more "Tony Corcarelli Originals" than he did? And what did that say about her?

He didn't care, couldn't care. Questions like that put him right back in the middle of senior year, and his high school philosophy elective, which he failed. No. Thank. You. So he stood, stretched and headed back to the kitchen for another beer. With any luck he'd get good and drunk, and forget everything.

Two steps from the fridge, the intercom buzzed.

Tony blinked at the clock above the stove, and then he glanced as his father's wristwatch, double-checking the time. Nobody would stop by this late. Must be a mistake, or an attempt to get in by somebody who shouldn't be getting in, so he ignored it, hoping they would move on to another sucker.

The intercom buzzed again.

Maybe it was the beer he'd guzzled while bone tired, but curiosity won out. He crossed the room and hit the button as the buzzer sounded a third time.

"Who is this?" he asked, sounding gruffer than he should, but hey, it was late, and it could still be someone up to no good.

Two heavy breaths echoed over the crackling line. "It's me, Trish."

Shit. All he could think about was her standing alone on his dark and dumpy street.

He hit the button extra hard. "Come on. Third floor." And then he met her on the stairs.

She was wrapped in a bright green raincoat, one that reminded him of the dress she wore to the wedding. Only the raincoat—and boots—covered every inch of flesh, especially when she clutched the collar tight at her neck.

Was it too much to hope for fishnets?

With her eyes wide and lips straight, she glanced up at him. "I hope you don't mind me stopping by."

He shrugged, still captured by the vision of her sweeping up his filthy stairs. "I'd say I'm surprised you didn't call first, but hey, that seems to be the norm around you." He grinned, and automatically slipped a hand beneath her elbow as she reached the landing. "Is everything okay?"

She blinked, nodded and then exhaled. "I think so."

An odd reply, odd enough for him to bite his tongue and lead her into his apartment before he asked any more questions. He closed the door behind them, and watched her walk into the center of the living area. She loosened her hold around her coat collar, letting it fall open at her throat. For some reason he stared at the pastel skin, like a man starving for a taste.

She touched a finger there, traced it back and forth along the faint line of bone. "This is...nice," she said.

"Don't lie." He didn't take his eyes off her finger, toying nervously, slipping in and out of the cover of her collar's hem. "It's shit. Certainly not a place for a woman like you." His voice faltered, scratching over the last few words. He wished he'd time to grab that second bottle of beer.

She flattened her palm against her chest, the tips of three fingers hidden beneath her collar and resting overtop her heart. "Me? Please. I've seen worse. And everything has potential. It's just a matter of seeing beyond the roughness."

Why did he feel like she was talking about him? His skin tightened and his mouth dried. He rubbed his fingers across the stubble on his jaw, desperate for something to say. "Can I get you a drink?"

"No." She shook her head. "I, uh, probably won't be staying long. I just wanted you to know that I told Angie I think I'm pregnant."

He didn't know which one of her statements bothered him more. One, that she wasn't planning on staying. Two, that Angie knew. Or three, that Trish thought she was pregnant. He rubbed his hand along his jaw again and then up over his face to his forehead. After a few more rubs, he said the first thing that came to mind. "What did Ange say?"

Trish laughed. "Let's just say she's promised to stay out of our business unless I ask for her help."

Tony didn't like the idea of Trish asking anyone but him for help, not when it came to their baby, their family, and he would've said so if he didn't realize he was getting way ahead of himself. "Are you pregnant?" He almost couldn't say the word, not because he didn't want her to be, but because the idea of her saying no had him breathing with his chest clamped.

"Technically it's still too soon to tell, but I'm feeling like I am. I don't know. Maybe I'm imagining it." She looked at the sofa behind her, and then sat.

He watched her shoulders rise and fall. Nonna wanted him to be happy. Tony wanted Nonna to be happy. Who'd have thought Trish having his baby could be the answer to both?

"If I am pregnant, Angie says you should marry me." Trish looked at him, those big eyes blazing. "I'm telling you right now that is not what I expect from you. I never expected that. I will go to bat for you with your family, because I know how traditional they can be. So no pressure, ya hear?" She blinked a few times, and then forced a smile.

Ya hear? Under normal circumstances he would have teased her about his lack of proper English rubbing off on her, but hey, they were talking about more than his poor grammar becoming a part of her. They were talking about his child. And marriage. And suddenly, all the silly, flirty games he lived to play whenever she rolled around didn't hold the same allure.

But marrying her did. If Trish was going to be the mother of his baby, then Angie was right. Tony needed to marry Trish, to give his baby legitimacy, a real last name, a dad who didn't come around once or twice a year, a dad who taught him how to fish, hold a hammer, stand up for the little guy and take care of the women who meant something, all things Tony's dad taught him.

His throat closed, but he cleared the way for words with an extra-deep breath. "What if I wanted to marry you?"

She tucked her chin to her chest and furrowed her brow. "Why would you want to do that? I mean, it's not like I'd ever try to keep you from the baby." She shrugged. "What's the benefit of going to such an extreme?"

Of course his juvenile brain jumped right to the honeymoon, causing him to grin.

"I'm serious, Tony. What would marriage do besides placate your family and tie us to a relationship that could get ugly? I don't want to raise a child with a man I hate." She stared at him with an intensity he'd come to expect, like she was trying to draw out the truth with a tractor beam radiating from her heart.

He lost the smile and walked toward her. "You could never hate me." If he had to, he would prove his point.

"It happens to the best of them," she said, wrinkling her nose.

"Did it happen with Stu?" Cards on the table, because the douche had been in and out of Tony's thoughts for too many days. Once and for all, he wanted to know where he stood.

Trish fidgeted as she loosened the belt around her waist. "No. Not at all. I'm indifferent to Stu. When we broke up, I was sad, but I wasn't heartbroken. There's a big difference."

Tony sat. "Oh yeah, what's the difference?"

She shuddered when she exhaled. "Sadness is in your head, not in your heart." And then she tapped a finger to her temple. "The stuff up here can be replaced by other stuff, sellout prices on bolts of fabric, minimum measurements for a master bath, that sort of thing." Her smile was shaky.

So he smiled back, but then he touched a finger to the slight bulge of her left breast, and neither one of them was smiling anymore. "What about the stuff in here?" he asked, smoothing his finger over the flawless skin. "What can that be replaced with?"

"Nothing," she said, swallowing loudly. "It just lives on, and on, wishing things could've turned out differently."

Yeah? Well, suddenly Tony wanted to be sure that things would be as different as they could ever be. He slipped his hand into the hair at the base of her head and gently tugged until she opened her mouth. And then he kissed her, erasing all thought of why she'd come and what she'd been doing here. This was all that mattered. He needed her, and if her hands strangling the fabric of his shirt were any indication, she needed him too. And not just to make a baby. Somehow this had turned into so much more.

Tony pushed into her, laying her down, spreading her coat around her body while he worked with his tongue inside her mouth. Wanting her burned him alive, had him squirming in his skin. He fumbled with the buttons of her shirt, yanking and twisting until one broke free and landed on the floor with a tap.

"No worries," he said, smiling against her lips. "I can fix that. There are benefits to a man who can sew."

She chuckled, wrapped her arms around his neck and pressed her bottom half to his. "After you fix the button, you should fix this couch."

He reared his head and narrowed his eyes, while his hand slipped beneath silky fabric to her breast. "What's wrong with this couch?"

"It's ugly," she said, hissing as he rolled her nipple, making it hard.

"Just for that, I'm going to keep you here—all night long."

Never once did she complain.

CHAPTER FIFTEEN

Trish stood in the Collins's remodeled kitchen behind a shiny metal island, propping her elbows on the acid-dyed concrete countertop. She scrolled through Google search results for *early pregnancy symptoms* on her phone. She should've had these memorized by now. Spotting? *Nope.* Cramping? *Yep.* Tender breasts? She cringed. *Oh yes!* Tired? Cranky? Nauseated? *Check. Check. Check.*

She hated to say it for fear of false hope, but it looked like her chances were good, especially now that she and Tony were having regular sex—two nights in a row and counting. The first night, on his couch. The second night, on hers. Tonight, maybe they'd make it to a bed.

She blushed, which was stupid. The nearest crewmember worked on the opposite side of the house. And even if they wandered by, they couldn't read her mind. Still, she absentmindedly fanned her face with her hand, hastening a return to normal, thinking maybe the blush signified nervousness instead of embarrassment.

After all, having more sex with Tony increased her chances of pregnancy, but it also increased her anxiety over what they meant to each other beyond the baby making, something that had boggled her mind since he didn't balk at the idea of marrying her. *Only if I'm pregnant*, she reminded herself. And because it was the honorable thing to do, like Angie said.

It wasn't like Tony professed his undying love for her. Besides, he hadn't mentioned marriage since the night at his place, and even then, he only mentioned it in passing. Maybe it was all about getting her into bed—or on the couch. She shook away a fresh batch of tingles crawling up her face.

She was too late to get control of this situation, wasn't she? A few months ago she would've sorted her feelings and made a plan by making a list of the pros and cons. She tapped her screen and opened a blank note, typing + *vs. – of recreational sex with Tony*, but then she stared at the electronic page, not a single bullet item, good or bad, forming in her head.

Pregnancy brain. *Check.*

Her phone chimed, and a text from Angie overtook the screen. *ETA 5 seconds.*

Straightening on an inhale, Trish deleted the note and tucked the phone into the pocket on her hip so she could meet the delivery truck at the door. As she watched the familiar van back into the driveway, her stupid heart thudded against her ribs, and her smile broadened.

Because Tony was driving.

Before Trish could get carried away with the anticipation of seeing him again, Angie leaped from the passenger side, steel-toed boots colliding with the pavers. She pointed to the Corcarelli Carpentry Co. logo over her left breast. "I must've forgotten how to read. Can you see if the word delivery or hauling is printed on here, because I'm confused. Every time I turn around he has me lugging something else, while my crew runs around million-dollar homes unsupervised."

Trish patted Angie's upper arm. "Your crew is behaving themselves beautifully."

Angie nodded, a rare smile splitting her face. "Music to my ears." She ripped the rubber band from her wrist and fastened her hair into a knot at her neck. "Seriously, though, who'd have thought garbage could weigh so freaking much?"

"It's not garbage," Tony said, rounding the front of the truck. "It's art." He said the words to Angie, but he was grinning at Trish. "Tell her, babe."

Apparently Trish had upgraded from Boss Lady. Of course she blushed, but she managed to keep her smile intact and speak. "It's art, and it's perfect. Exactly what I wanted."

143

"Cripes," Angie said. "If I were in middle school, I'd be gagging myself with my finger, but since I'm all grown up and running a business here, I'll forego the antics so we can *work*. Tony, if you can peel your eyes off of her for ten freaking minutes, then we can haul this trash inside."

Angie clomped to the back of the truck, while Tony sauntered to Trish.

"Hey," he said, widening his grin and looping his arm around her waist.

She was just about to protest when he pulled her against him, and thrilled her with a hard, hot kiss.

"Tony, so help me God…" Angie's voice mixed with the truck's clanging, rolling rear door.

Tony didn't seem to care. His arms tightened around Trish's waist, and she had to push palms to his chest to gain release.

"You should go before she gets angry," Trish whispered.

"She's always angry," he replied loud enough for Angie to hear, and then he placed a kiss on Trish's nose and joined his sister inside the truck.

Trish wandered after them, warmed by his kiss. Was this really her life, thriving design company, hot male companion who made marriage seem appealing, and a baby on the way? It sounded like a fairytale.

"Boss, we got a problem." Nico Corcarelli held open the front door. "You need to call the plumber. Mickey hit the main line."

That was when Trish remembered she never held much stock in fairytales. Real life got messy. Planning and preparing weren't guarantees. Angie's crew had blueprints and hashmarks, and still they had hit the line. Trish's lists had pros and cons, and still some things fit both sides. She hated that, wished there was some way to control the chaos. But when she found herself standing ankle-deep in tap water, the only thing she could hope for was to be strong enough that chaos couldn't wash her away.

• • •

"Can I stay?" Tony dragged his lips from Trish's lobe to follow her jawline.

Since the Collins's family room flooded, she'd been preoccupied. Tony hoped a little lovin' would put her body and mind to rest, but she had yet to reciprocate his advances, so he figured he better ask, being a gentleman and all.

Technically, she wasn't his "woman" to be pawing anyway.

"If you want." She fidgeted beside him on her living room couch.

He winced and sat up, giving her some space. "Do *you* want? 'Cause right now it doesn't seem like you want me here."

She sighed. "I'm sorry. I have a lot on my mind."

"Like?"

"Work. You were there. You saw the mess."

"It's being professionally cleaned."

"But it's a setback and more dollar signs." She ran her fingers through her shiny hair, tugging on a clump when she reached the ends. "And then there's this." She patted her stomach. "Am I? Am I not? It's a constant back and forth."

He slid his arm along the back of the sofa, lifting his hand to play with her hair.

"And then there's this." She gestured at his hand.

Tony froze with a strand wrapped around his index finger. "What? This?" He tugged the strand.

"Yes." She lifted her shoulders and shuddered.

"What about this?" He dropped his hand to her head and rubbed.

"What is this?" She shrugged again, this time acting an awful lot like she wanted to be free of him.

He could take a hint. "A massage," he said, dropping his hand and sliding a few inches away.

"That's not what I meant. I'm sorry. I'm…" she sighed and shook her head. "Maybe it's the hormones making me cranky."

"Maybe. Or maybe you're realizing you don't like me as much as you thought you did." It didn't sound like the joke he meant for it to be. He leaned forward, embarrassed he sounded so needy.

"No." She flattened a hand against his back. "That's definitely not it."

The heat from her hand seeped beneath his skin, warming his blood until his breathing quickened. "Good," was all he could manage to say.

"I just feel a lot of pressure, and I worry it's somehow going to end badly, you know?"

He nodded. Despite the great sex and his strange lack of horror at the thought of marrying Trish, he could relate to her worry. Hard not to, with Angie warning him daily of the potential for doom. Two days ago, she backed him against the tool cabinet in her garage and threatened to castrate him if he fucked up. Talk about pressure.

"And the more we carry on like this, the more I worry we're kidding ourselves that we'll be able to be objective if…" her hand dropped from his back, "I'm not pregnant, and Nonna…" She huffed. "I'm sorry."

Glancing over his shoulder at her bunched face, he reached across the cushion and took her hand. "Don't be. Nothin' to be sorry about. You're a thinker. That's a good thing. I should probably do a little more of that."

She shrugged, but then settled into tracing her thumb over his knuckle. He liked the way her hand looked smaller in his. "Thinking is good," she said. "Overthinking is not. There should be a balance."

He straightened, moving closer, keeping her hand wrapped in his. "Like you should feel as much as you think?"

"Exactly."

He wanted to kiss her again. "I can help with that, you know?" He lifted her hand from his lap and placed it on his chest as he moved in for that kiss. 'If you want me to."

"I do," she said, tickling his lips with her whisper.

And he did.

After two nights of half-hearted sleep on surprisingly uncomfortable couches, Tony hauled Trish to bed. Of course, they didn't sleep much once they got there either, and that sort of bothered him. He slipped out of bed, making a mental note to Google *sex during pregnancy* before he kept her up again.

While she slept, bathed in moonlight, he showered and brushed his teeth with the spare toothbrush she magically produced the night before. It only partially wigged him out that she kept it in the holder next to hers.

Without waking her, he headed downstairs for coffee. Two nights and days in a row, and somehow it felt like routine. All he needed was a change of clothes and it'd be like he was living here.

The thought stopped him on the bottom stair. He glanced around the flashy, floral surroundings lit by the soft glow of the crown molding lights. Hardly what he'd call his style, but damn, he liked that sixty-inch TV. And the bed. And the family room couch. Hell, every piece of upholstered furniture here.

That thought got him moving again, eyeing each piece he'd created. Some of his best work lived in this house. He swelled with pride, and then he thought about his child, being raised here, climbing all over that couch. Something sparked beneath his breast.

The spark lingered, even after a lightning-quick bike ride to his apartment through the dark and driving rain. Hours later, in the late of day, standing in the middle of Angie's garage, the flash of feeling only intensified. The next thing he knew, he was sketching plans for a rocking chair. Suddenly, nothing seemed more important than taking care of Trish and his kid.

"I'm headed over to Nonna's. You wanna come?"

Tony looked up from the sketches and blinked a few times to clear his head. Somebody else was pretty damn important. "Yeah. I do."

Angie nodded, glancing at the papers pressed beneath his hands. "You ready now?"

"Yep," he said, folding the papers and stuffing them into his pocket.

"Top secret plans?"

"Maybe."

Angie narrowed her eyes as she hit the button, raising the garage door. "Would you show me if I asked?"

"No. You called my table trash." He fell in step beside her as she walked to her car.

"I was kidding."

"You hurt my feelings."

"You're an ass."

When they were both inside the car, she gripped his headrest and narrowed her eyes again. "Show me."

"Why?"

"Because I'm curious."

"You're nosy."

"Whatever. Same thing."

Tony propped his elbow on the door and stared at the basketball hoop missing its net outside the window. "They're plans for a chair."

She started the engine and backed the car from the drive. "For Nonna?"

Tony closed his eyes and rested his forehead against his palm. He'd been hoping his family wouldn't ask questions about his contribution to the list. Chaos surrounding Nonna's decline bought him some time, but not enough. With Vin's concert at the end of the week, the list had once again become the family's favorite topic.

"Yeah, sorta," he said, partly to get Angie off his back, and partly because it was true. The chair might be for Trish and the baby, but as far as he was concerned, the baby was for Nonna.

"What kind of chair?"

"Ange, forget about it. You'll see it when everyone else sees it."

"I'll see it as soon as you start working on it, dork. My garage is your workshop. Remember?"

He dropped a fist to the vinyl-clad door.

"Is it a recliner?"

"No."

"A wing chair?"

"No." She wasn't going to let it go. "Fine. It's a rocking chair," he said, none too happy he caved.

She nodded, eyes never shifting from the road. She drove a few blocks before she spoke again. "Maybe she'll rock the baby to sleep."

Tony looked at her long enough to notice a single unshed tear, gathering at the corner of her lashes. "Maybe," he said with the image clogging his throat.

It was amazing how the separate pieces of his life had become so intertwined.

CHAPTER SIXTEEN

Trish stretched her arms behind her back and struggled with the gown's zipper. If only her breasts weren't aching monstrosities…If only Tony had brought his dress clothes with him when he spent the night…Then, she wouldn't be having this problem. She'd have help with the zipper instead.

She glanced at the mounds of flesh screaming for release from the heart neckline. "No," she snapped, forcing the zipper up her back, much to her bosom's chagrin.

There was no way she was going to wear something comfortable and sensible to Nonna's concert. Trish smoothed a hand over the bodice of the black satin dress. If she was as pregnant as she suspected she was, then this would be the last time she could squeeze into this blessed thing.

Leaning forward for a closer look in the bathroom mirror, she wrapped a thin strand of hair around her index finger and doused the spring with hairspray, careful not to breathe the fumes. She did the same thing on the other side, and then walked to her closet where a silver clutch perched on a shelf. *Big enough for tampons*, she thought. And immediately she followed the thought with a frown. She hated planning for both outcomes, but what was the alternative, blindly believing she was pregnant and ending up a mess at the concert? She shuddered. No way. Besides, she was being proactive, not negative. Carrying supplies wasn't tantamount to a jinx.

Nodding twice for good measure, Trish swiped the purse from the shelf and filled it with lipstick, tissues, and a tampon. Then, she slipped into silver strappy heels.

"Not fair. Not fair."

The smooth voice echoing in the bathroom made Trish smile. She glanced over her shoulder and batted her lashes at a grinning Tony. "I don't know what you're talking about."

He wrapped around her from behind, nuzzling his lips against her neck. "You were supposed to wait for me to get back so I could zip you."

She giggled. "Uh huh, I can only imagine how that would've ended up."

"With this dress on the floor," he said, sliding his hands over her waist and hips, and then up over her breasts.

She flinched. "Careful."

He lightened the touch of his hands and the pressure of his lips. "Still sore?"

"Still sore." She worried about the resounding hope in her voice.

"That's a good sign, right?"

"Right," she answered, worrying about the resounding hope in his voice even more.

For a week now, they'd been living on the fumes of the hypothetical. If she was pregnant...If they got married...But they were building a house of cards. One negative test, and it would scatter.

Of course, they could try again, they would try again—as long as Nonna hung around. But there were no guarantees of that. And then what? Would Tony hang around and continue to play this game just so Trish could have a baby? She hated to think he wouldn't. Each night they spent together led to another morning with Trish staring at the ceiling wondering who she wanted more: the baby or Tony.

He turned her in his arms, pressing her body to his, brushing his lips over her forehead. "You look beautiful."

She smiled, taking her mind off her worry by admiring him. She'd seen the slim fit suit before, how the sleek black wool kissed every angle of his body, how the crisp white cotton shirt contrasted against his tanned throat. And yet each and every time she saw him dressed like this, she melted.

"You look beautiful, too." Trish rolled onto her toes and craned her neck, placing her lips along his jaw, tasting the spice of his aftershave, breathing him into her soul.

She didn't want just any baby. She wanted his baby. Because she wanted him. Period. The revelation forced her onto flat feet, where she stared at him like a lovesick fool. *Love.*

A little sound escaped her lips.

"What?"

"Nothing. I…the dress is tight, I guess."

He grinned, glancing down at her overflowing neckline. "I like it tight."

"I'm sure you do." She swatted him to tease, but also to gain some distance.

Love was not part of her plan. Like? Yes. Respect? Absolutely. She wanted to co-parent with someone she could tolerate. The all-consuming attraction complicated things, but she figured that would fade. After all, how hot could he be for her when she was thirty pounds heavier with swollen feet, unshaved legs, and her face buried in a half-gallon of Rocky Road?

And how hot could she be for him when he was taking off on his motorcycle or throwing back a couple beers while she was walking the floors with a colicky newborn? Attraction would definitely fade, and then they would be left with common sense and commonalities like the baby, Angie, and work. But love? *Crap.* Love changed everything, especially if it was one-sided.

"We should get going. Vin said absolutely, positively nobody gets in late."

Trish flashed a smile at Tony in the bathroom mirror. "Uh huh." There was so much more to say, but there wasn't time to say it, especially since what she wanted to say could rip their heads from the clouds and drive a wedge between them. *Love?* She had a feeling that one word would have Tony Corcarelli running away.

"You okay?" He slipped a hand across her lower back.

"Yep." But she'd be better once she took a pregnancy test and she knew where they stood.

...

Tony looked around the Hillman Center lobby, wondering how Vin planned to uphold his no-late-admissions policy, considering the guest of honor was the one who was late. He'd be worried if Angie hadn't just arrived, saying Ma, Aunt Connie, and Nonna were on their way. He'd be even more worried if Trish's hand wasn't nearby to hold. Having her here, with him, made him mellow.

"You need to clean up the garage. I swear if I trip over another tool, I'm going to beat you with it, and then I'm kicking you out," Angie said.

The harsh words made him smile, considering they were delivered by a woman who could be considered a knockout if she wasn't his pain-in-the-ass, know-it-all sister.

It was nice to know things were back to normal.

"How are you feeling?" Angie whispered to Trish.

Okay, so things weren't exactly back to normal.

"I'm good," Trish said, but when she smiled, the expression didn't reach her eyes.

Tony wondered what was bothering her. He wondered if Angie caught on to the fib, too. This was a new kind of normal. Him, with Trish, knowing her well enough to decipher clues to her mood. Trish, with him, carrying his baby. Surreal, for sure, but normal now, too. He touched a hand to the small of her back and then cupped her waist, moving her closer.

"Attention, everyone," Vin called over the crowd from his perch on the staircase. "We're going to go ahead and open the house, so you can be seated. As soon as Nonna arrives, we'll start."

He looked like hell, collar crooked, deep wrinkles marring his shirt. Tony had a hunch some serious pit stains lurked beneath that suit coat. "He's going to have a heart attack before he's fifty."

Angie swatted Tony's arm. "Did you ever think of helping him? This is a big deal. He planned this all by himself."

"With minimal help from the girls in his office, I'm sure." Tony shot Angie his don't-give-me-any-of-your-bullshit look, but then he smiled and winked.

She wrinkled her nose. "Fine, then I'll ask if he needs help." She stormed away.

"You can go, you know? I'll be okay." Trish's head followed Angie's path through the crowd.

"I don't want to go," Tony whispered against her ear. "Why would I leave the most beautiful woman in the room? Somebody's bound to make a move."

She pushed a palm against his chest, but then she gripped his lapel, leaning into him. They stayed that way, wrapped in a hug, while the rest of the Corcarelli clan filtered into the auditorium. A few cousins waggled their brows as they passed. One even gave thumbs up. Warmth fizzed in Tony's chest. Approval from his family definitely felt weird.

He smiled overtop Trish's head at the last cousin to leave the lobby, and then he kissed her temple. "We should sit."

Her grip tightened on his lapel. "I have to...use the lady's room." And then she left him to watch her erratic steps as her ankles wobbled in the too-high heels.

The warmth in his chest turned ice cold, causing him to rub a hand over his heart.

"Tony, hold the door."

He blinked, shook his head, and then turned toward his mother's voice. She was poking around the jamb of the exit door. A horrible sound, like a sick dog barking, filtered into the lobby from behind her. He didn't ask whose dog. He didn't care. He simply rushed forward, taking the edge of the door from her hand.

The barking grew louder as Ma and Aunt Connie helped a coughing Nonna into the building.

Tony pulled his brows together above his nose. "Hey, Nonna."

Her eyes rolled in his direction, and her lips twitched, but another cough foiled her smile and words.

He looked at his mother, who was shaking her head in a not-now motion. "We're late. Vinnie's going to have our heads." She offered a quick smile as the small group shuffled toward the auditorium door.

There had to be more to her tension than punctuality.

Out of the corner of his eye, Tony saw Trish emerge from the ladies room. She smiled at him, a gesture that injected relief into his veins. Then, she stumbled when she saw the other women.

"Hello," she said, offering a little wave with her shiny purse.

Tony watched his mother and aunt smile in return, but then Nonna coughed again, and all attention gravitated to her. Something told him to go to Trish, to let Nonna see them together. At first, he balked. He'd spent most of his life ignoring his conscience's little guilt trips where his family was concerned. That didn't feel like the right thing to do anymore.

Crossing the lobby, he took Trish by the hand. "Nonna, you remember Trish DeVign, don't you?"

Nonna stopped, eyes on Trish and Tony's interlocking hands. She shook her elbow until Ma released her, and then she did the same to Aunt Connie. "I remember," she said. Every syllable soaked in breath. She coughed as she reached both hands into the air, taking Tony by the left cheek and Trish by the right.

A lump formed in Tony's chest. Nonna didn't have the strength to squeeze, but the gesture was powerful nonetheless.

"Good," she managed before dropping her hands on another coughing fit.

"Mother, you need to sit," Aunt Connie said.

Vin burst through the auditorium doors. "There you are." He took Nonna's face in his hands and kissed her nose before he accepted her hand from Tony's mother. "Let's get this show on the road."

Ma fell behind, into step with Tony and Trish. "It's the fluid," she whispered. "Again. Only it's worse. Connie and I tried to get her to let us take her to the ER. She's so stubborn."

Ma moved ahead when Nonna coughed again.

The coughing attracted the attention of the rest of the family. One by one, they turned in their seats, smiles on their lips but fear in their eyes.

Tony knew the feeling.

Trish squeezed his hand, and somehow that helped enough to get him down the aisle to his seat and through the first set of songs despite Nonna's coughing.

But nothing helped when Vin cancelled the second set to call an ambulance.

• • •

Trish moved through the crowded lobby, desperate to reach the ladies room before anyone stopped her. For the second time today, she suspected her period. There couldn't be a worse time for obsessing over this.

Pushing against the swinging door, she blinked back tears and walked to the farthest stall. The tears were for Nonna, she told herself, not for what may or may not happen in here. Life vs.

death? Hardly a contest. Besides, if she wasn't pregnant now, she could try again.

The blood-tinged pantyliner caught her eye at the exact time Angie's voice echoed in her ear.

"Trish, you in here?"

Maybe if she didn't so much as breathe.

"Hey, Tony sent me to grab you. We're going to head over to Vin's to wait on news."

"I..." her voice caught, "need a second." Her stomach pushed into her throat. "Maybe two."

Angie's heels tapped against the tile floor until she was standing outside the stall. "You okay?"

"Yes." No, but how could she cry to Angie about not being pregnant when Nonna was losing the battle? Trish had other chances. Nonna might not. Still...

"You don't sound okay."

"I'm fine." She lifted her gaze to the ceiling and exhaled. "I'll be out soon."

Angie huffed. "If you say so..." The heels tapped the tile as she walked away. "See you at Vin's." The door shut behind her, and Trish was left in the blessed silence of her tears.

She wasn't pregnant, and Nonna was gravely ill. Maybe everything was hopeless.

Somehow, Trish managed to take care of herself and exit the stall, all the while wondering how she'd tell Tony, when she'd tell him, certainly not today, not until he knew Nonna was okay—if she was okay.

Acid burned Trish's chest and throat. An hour ago, she would've thought it a sign of pregnancy. Now, she knew better, and better sucked.

Standing at the sink, washing her hands, Trish stared bleary-eyed into the mirror until Tony appeared.

"Hey." His beautiful smile faded when he saw her, and then his face bunched with concern.

"I'm not pregnant." She hadn't planned to tell him this way. It wasn't timely. It wasn't eloquent. But she needed to say it out loud so she could move on. Somehow saying it to his reflection proved easier.

He closed his eyes, briefly, but it was long enough to add the weight of his disappointment to her already sagging shoulders.

"I'm sorry," she said as sobs forced from her chest. "I wanted to help you. I wanted to…"

"Awe, babe." He walked to her, wrapped her in his arms and kissed her head. "We'll try again. That's all there is to it."

His simple, perfect answer caused more tears, and then a question hounded her brain. "Why? Why do you want to try again?" Maybe if he said he loved her, the pain of losing the baby she'd dreamed of this time would go away.

He stared at her reflection. "You're upset. Let's take a minute to get you cleaned up and calmed down."

"I just…" She sniffed against his chest, wanting to tell him she loved him. But hadn't she burdened him with enough confessions today?

A noise in the lobby grabbed his attention, and he loosened his grip on her shoulders, leaning closer to the door. "We need to get to Vin's. I'm sorry. I…"

He was worried about Nonna, too. She couldn't—shouldn't—compete with that.

"No. No. I know." She sniffed, trying her damnedest to get control of the disappointment. "You need to get to Vin's."

He cupped her cheeks and lifted her face to him. "It's all going to be okay."

She shook her head. "I know." But she didn't know anything. Right now okay seemed like a longshot. "You should go."

His brows bunched together. "I thought...you would come, too."

"That was before this." She prayed for the words to be sure and strong. "I'm a mess. I don't have what I need to be someplace else for the long haul, and I need to get out of this dress. You understand, don't you?"

He nodded, but the brows remained tied. "Then I'll drive you home. You can change and get what you need."

"No." She pushed away from him as noises in the lobby filtered through the louvered cracks in the door. "Go, Tony. Your family needs you. I'm fine. I really, truly am." Liar, liar, but she was better than Nonna, and that's where his focus needed to be.

His dark eyes widened on a lift of his chin. "I don't like leaving you like this. It's wrong."

"Not if I tell you to go. I'm not dying, Tony. I got my period." Could she have been a bigger bitch? Nausea, big and bold, turned her stomach inside out. Another symptom of her non-existent pregnancy.

He nodded slowly, reaching into his coat pocket and pulling out her keys. "Okay then, I guess I'll ride with Ange." When she didn't hold out her hand to accept the keys, he placed them on the counter. "I'll call you, to let you know how she is." And then he was gone.

Trish stood there, frozen against the bathroom sink, listening to the fading sounds outside the door. When she finally pushed into the empty lobby reality hit her.

Two years spent plotting and planning for a biological family, and she'd never been more alone.

CHAPTER SEVENTEEN

"Where's Trish?"

Angie's question wasn't one Tony cared to answer, so he ignored her, staring at the horse on the dashboard of her '65 Mustang instead.

"I went into that bathroom, remember. I know something was wrong. Is she sick?"

Why were the women in his life so damn nosy, and why did he feel this obligation to keep the peace by giving in? No wonder he ran every chance he got for so many years. It was easier than hanging around and being badgered by them.

"Tony?"

"She got her period. Okay? Cripes." It was easier to word it that way than to say she wasn't pregnant.

"Oh. Maybe that's a good thing."

He heard his patience snap. It sounded like ears popping from too much pressure in his head. "A good thing? Seriously? No, Ange. It's not a good thing. It's a terrible thing, a fucking awful thing. That baby meant something…to Trish."

"Sounds like it meant something to you, too."

She was not going to bait him again. "Whatever. I'm gonna try callin' Aunt Connie again." How shitty was his life that he was distracting himself from bad news with even worse news?

Of course, she didn't pick up.

"It's a hospital, Tony. She has it on vibrate, which means we won't talk to anyone until they call us. Settle down."

And talk about Trish? No thank you. So he'd stick with the next worst thing. "Why does the fluid make Nonna cough?"

Angie shrugged. "Vin did some research on his phone while we waited in the lobby. He said it could be building up in her chest cavity. I don't know what it's called. Some fancy name."

"I don't care what it's called, either. I just wanna know if it means the cancer is spreading?"

She shrugged again. "All I know is they can drain fluid from her chest like they've been draining it from her abdomen. She'll get some relief then. Let's focus on that."

Tony pressed fingertips against his eyelids until the pressure hurt, and then he whacked his head off the headrest a couple times. He didn't want to focus on anything, because everything sucked.

He opened his mouth to tell Angie to swing by Trish's house so he could grab his bike, then he could ride far and fast as soon as he knew Nonna was comfortable. He could also check on Trish, make sure she was okay.

But what if she wasn't? He closed his mouth without saying a word. If Trish was upset, he wouldn't want to leave. It'd be the same feeling he'd felt when they were alone in the restroom, like he was being torn apart.

"You know, up until today I couldn't figure out why she was with you."

Tony sort of glared at his sister, knowing exactly which "she" she was talking about. Was it too much to ask for her not to analyze this relationship? Heck, Tony was still trying to figure out exactly what it had become. Maybe Angie figured out what brought Tony and Trish together in the first place—Trish's baby-making plan. It was definitely too much to ask for Angie to think it possible that Trish was with him because he was worthy of her.

"You're different with her, you know?" Angie continued. "How you hold her hand and look at her, all that touchy-feely crap I've never seen you do with anyone. And she talks to you, more than she talks to me, which is warped, but also a good sign. I mean, it must mean you're good to her...for her." The wrinkles on her face tightened. "Blah, blah, blah." She lifted her hands from the wheel, waved them in front of her like she was erasing the sentiments, and then shot him a shitty grin.

Well, color him surprised. Part of him wanted to thank her, but that much emotion between them would've been plain weird. "I don't know about all that," he said, trying to play it off.

"Well, how 'bout we say you have moments? And the last thing I'm ever going to say about it is she's good for you, too."

Tony had less of a problem agreeing with that, but he didn't say so. Saying it would've made him miss her even more. Inhaling, he focused on the blazing ball of sun rising above the U.S. Steel Tower.

"What I'm trying to say is, you're here, and that's…something."

He caught Angie's insinuation, that Trish was somehow the reason for him not bailing on this family vigil, like he'd bailed on every one when Dad was sick. Maybe Tony being here did mean something, but he was too worried about the women he loved to analyze it.

Not until Angie parked in Vin's packed driveway did Tony's thoughts catch up with him. He was here, because he was worried about Nonna. He loved her. And if he wasn't here, he'd be with Trish, because he loved her, too. He had to. He couldn't imagine life without her by his side.

Baby or no baby, he wanted to be with Trish DeVign.

His jaw dropped, and he feigned an itch so he could scratch his chin and manually close his gaping mouth.

He was in love?

Vin was going to shit.

Now what? He leaned closer to the passenger door, hoping Angie didn't catch onto his erratic breathing. If he told Trish how he felt, she might not feel the same. But what if she did? What if all the hypotheticals could be real?

Tony didn't know what shocked him more, that he managed to fall in love or that he wanted hypotheticals that included marriage.

Marriage. He couldn't think of anything better than being hitched to Trish, waking up to her day after day, making love to her night after night, and laughing with her every moment in between.

As soon as the Nonna situation was under control, he was going to find Trish and tell her.

• • •

Trish stared at the telephone, wanting to call Tony. But when she picked up the phone, she wondered if she shouldn't call Angie instead. Maybe she'd pushed him too hard. Maybe he wasn't calling for a reason.

Like maybe there's no news. Of course, that could be true.

She slid the pain reliever off the counter and popped four into her mouth, swallowing them without a drop of water. They caught in her throat for a few seconds, and for those few blissful seconds, she thought of something other than the Corcarellis. But then she swallowed the pills completely, and the worry for Nonna and questions about Tony returned. Trish might not be a Corcarelli by blood, but lately the family had consumed her. In some ways, she felt like she belonged more to them than to her adoptive parents.

Curling up on the couch, Trish lifted her phone and this time dialed her mother, the woman who used to put her to sleep with stories about adoption being love by choice, not by accident.

The older Trish got, the more she resented the reminder that she came into this world an accident, and the more she forgot about how powerful a choice could be. She needed to make the choice to appreciate her mother for what she did give, because love was never easy.

"Hello." Delores sounded like she answered the phone following a five-mile run. Trish trampled the impulse to assume the breathlessness meant her mother didn't have time for her. She'd done enough overthinking for one day.

"Hi. I thought you might want to know they had to rush Tony and Angie's grandmother to the hospital."

"Oh my. I'm sorry to hear that. Which hospital, dear? I'll have an arrangement sent with a card. Are you doing something on your own or should I include you?"

"I'll do something on my own."

"Fine, dear." There was a pause, and then a sigh. "Something else is wrong, isn't there?"

"Nothing as important or serious as Nonna."

"Work?"

"It's good."

Another sigh, like it was hard for her to even think about her next words. "And Tony?"

"It's complicated." Even more complicated than having this conversation with her mother.

"Well, I think…"

"Mother, I already know what you think, and it's time you know what I think." Trish sucked a big breath into her lungs. "I love him. I don't know how it's going to turn out, but me loving him isn't going to change." She expected the shocked silence. "I just wanted you to know."

"Does he love you?"

The phone chimed in Trish's ear and vibrated in her hand. She pulled it back far enough to see Tony's name flashing on the screen. "I gotta go. That's him with news about Nonna."

In the seconds that it took to disconnect one call and connect with the other, there wasn't relief over avoiding her mother's question so much as there was resignation at what the answer would be. Trish loved Tony, like it or not, and whether or not he loved her.

"Hey, how is she?" Trish asked without the customary hello, wanting to get straight to the point before she said something stupid.

"Better. They're draining the fluid."

"Good." And it was good, good that Nonna was feeling better and good to hear his voice.

"How are you?"

She smiled, because at least he cared. "Better, too."

"You up for company?"

Her heart flipped. "Sure." But then she heard the ruckus in the background. "I don't want to take you from your family."

He was quiet longer than necessary, unless he was struggling with where he wanted to be.

"I could...come there," she babbled. "If you wanted me... needed me to."

"Okay."

Their breathing filled the line, and a feeling of importance overwhelmed her. Occasionally in life, when you made the right decision, it pummeled you. "I'll be there soon."

By the time Trish reached Vin's, the moon glistened on the river. Cars filled the drive and lined the street in both directions. She rounded the corner and parked a block away, thankful she wore ballet flats instead of heels. As she approached the house, the shadow of an open car door and two outstretched legs caught her eye. A few more steps and she could see it was Angie.

"If you're going in there, you're in for a wild ride," Angie said, poking her face in the V of space created by the open door. "Look at me, hiding. Shit." Her exhale echoed in the night. "I just needed air."

"I thought everything was okay?" Trish stood in front of Angie who was sitting sideways in the driver's seat—barefoot—heels tipped over on the pavement.

"I guess it's okay, if okay is nobody ever knowing how long it's going to go on. Some jackass in the ER told my mother three more months."

Trish's heart seized.

"But, hell, they told my dad he had six months and he lived two years. So who knows? It's all a fucking crap shoot." She punched the door. "I hate dice games."

Which was an understatement. Trish once saw Angie whip a pair of dice across the table at a dealer from the local casino who told her she was hot. Hot, as in winning. Didn't matter to Angie.

The memory brought a smile to Trish's face, and then as if Angie was reading her mind, Angie smiled, too.

"I swear to God he was looking at my boobs that whole night," Angie sneered. "Jerk."

And they laughed, because, by God, someone needed to.

When the hysteria died, Angie bent at the waist and picked up her shoes. "You should go find Tony. He's new to this whole group worry thing. When I snuck out he was trapped in the kitchen between Aunt Helen and Uncle Giacomo. He may have stuffed his head in the oven by now."

Trish chuckled again. "What about you?"

"I think I'm going to go…for a ride, at least…just to clear my head."

Trish loved Angie and Tony too much to point out how the tables had turned.

A few minutes later, Trish stood on Vin's front porch, watching Angie drive away. When the taillights faded, she faced the door, her gaze zipping from knob to bell. She should ring, right? She wasn't family. Then again she was invited, expected. Tony asked her here.

"If you already rang, they probably didn't hear you." She turned toward the gravelly voice and the large man strolling up the drive. He barely fit between the rows of parked cars. "Or they're lazy. Probably the latter."

"I didn't ring." She followed the glowing cigarette Vin tossed to the ground.

He crushed the ember under his dress shoe. "Do me a favor. Don't tell Ange about that. She'll tell my ma, and then I'll never hear the end. It's not a habit. It's a crutch. Big difference."

Trish smiled, nodded and moved aside as he stepped onto the porch.

"He'll be happy to see you."

The random statement gave Trish some much needed courage. "I hope so."

Vin smiled in return. "I know so. He looks kind of lost without you."

Was it fair to wish it true, in spite of the reason they were gathering here?

Desperate to not overthink things, Trish followed Vin through the spotty crowd. She waved and smiled where it seemed to fit, but mostly she blended in as she moved toward the back of the house.

Tony was standing where Angie had left him between a scowling aunt and a clearly inebriated uncle.

He saw her and fled, meeting her in the hallway that linked the family room and kitchen.

"Shoot me dead." He gripped her by the upper arms and then shook his head. "Wait, bad joke. I didn't mean that." He exhaled. "It's just not my usual scene."

And still he was here. "I'm proud of you for staying."

"Yeah, well somebody had to. Angie bolted, then Vin." His lips hitched like he wasn't completely annoyed with the pair. Maybe because he was pleased with himself.

"Vin's back," Trish pointed out.

"Good, then he can listen to why Aunt Helen's anise balls are better than Aunt Vi's. And he can make Uncle G a vodka tonic that doesn't 'taste like piss.'" He drew quotation marks in the air.

"I love you." It barreled out like a simple expression meant to celebrate his sense of humor in difficult situations. But it was so much more. Her heart froze mid-beat, but then he started it again with a smile.

"You love me because I make a weak vodka tonic?"

"No." Heat picked at her face, and she found relief in a few stray tears. "I have my reasons. Good reasons, but I don't want to do this here."

He nodded, widened his smile and slipped a hand to her waist. "Okay. Fair enough." Leaning closer, his lips barely touched her ear. "For what it's worth, I love you, too, but you're right, let's not do this here."

"Tony, can you open this?" A preteen girl bounded toward them with a jar of giardiniera in hand. "Aunt Helen wants to see if it's as good as hers."

Tony opened the jar, all the while shaking his head. "Family. You sure you want to be a part of this?" he asked Trish as the child walked away.

How many ways could one woman say yes?

EPILOGUE

Tony adjusted the volume on the sixty-inch screen so his cousin's younger kids could hear the movie without waking the baby. On his way back into the living room, he snagged a couple beers from the fridge, one for Angie and one for Vin. He kissed his mother on the cheek, winked at Aunt Connie, and swiped a finger full of icing off the anise birthday cake.

Two steps inside the hallway, Mario stood whining at the top of the basement stairs. "Something's wrong with the pinball machine."

"I'll be right there, bud, making deliveries." He lifted the beers as proof.

Passing through the center hall, he stepped into the living room where most of the family gathered.

"I swear she looks like great-grandpa Leo. She's got that wide Romano nose."

Tony snarled at Aunt Josie. "Watch your mouth. Her nose is perfect."

"Down, Daddy," Vin said, grinning as he reached out to take a beer. "Nobody said it wasn't."

"She's certainly got her mother's eyes," Aunt Carmella said. "Corcarelli eyes are brown."

"They'll change," Trish offered from her spot on the couch. "Between six months and nine months, we should start to get an idea of what they're going to be."

Tony passed the other beer to Angie and then made his way to the empty spot next to his fiancée. He wasn't going to say it now, but he hoped Angelina did get her mother's eyes. Looking at them sparkling now, they were the most beautiful eyes he'd ever seen.

"Hey," he whispered, leaning in for a kiss. "You sure you don't need anything?"

"No, I'm good. Getting a much needed break." Trish smiled at the corner of the room.

Angelina had a strong attachment to Mommy. In fact, only one other person had the right rhythm to rock her to sleep.

"You okay over there, Nonna?" Tony asked, raising his voice enough for her to hear.

The thin but feisty woman gave her turban-covered head a hearty nod, never once breaking her rocking and patting beat.

"As soon as the baby wakes, we're going to sing and have cake." Ma stood behind the couch.

Nonna wrinkled her nose as if to say, who needed cake? She was right, Tony thought. His baby girl was even sweeter than a piece of Nonna's birthday cake—and that was saying something.

Tony gripped Trish's hand, pulling it into his lap. "I can't believe she made it to eighty-six."

A warm hand landed on his right shoulder, and he looked over his left shoulder to see Ma, her head fitting into the space between him and Trish.

"You two did this for her. You gave her a reason to live."

While Ma patted his shoulder and Trish squeezed his hand, Tony smiled.

They almost gave Nonna a setback by picking a wedding date after the baby's birth. After a few days of tears and a couple hundred laps on the rosary beads, she calmed down, and it didn't hurt they named the baby after her.

Nobody knew how much longer the cancer's slower progression would last. Tony was just happy it lasted long enough to get her here. He watched Nonna, rocking Angelina in the chair he'd made, and he thought he might be dreaming. He felt that way every morning waking up next to Trish.

Who'd have thought Tony Corcarelli would've turned into a family man?

• • •

Trish placed the swaddled, wide-eyed baby in the middle of the king-sized bed, and then pushed the comforter and pillows out of reach. Even though she had no intention of letting the baby sleep in this bed, it was better to be safe than sorry. She smiled, certain she was overthinking again. But when it came to Angelina, she gave herself a pass.

Satisfied the baby was safe, Trish settled onto the mattress and propped her head in her hand. This round-faced cherub child was hers. It still didn't seem real. Trish brushed a finger over the black fuzz, covering Angelina's head—she was Tony's too.

Tears rode the bumps of Trish's smiling cheeks. "Hi, baby girl. Watcha looking at?"

Angelina's wobbly gaze wandered toward Trish's voice.

"She's looking at the most beautiful woman in the world," Tony said, strolling into the bedroom from the hall. He was dressed in his clothes from the party, but his shirttails hung loose, and a dishtowel was draped over his shoulder.

"Daddy's too tired to see straight," Trish said to the baby.

Since the birth, Tony had been going overboard with compliments. She appreciated them, but exhausted, sporadically-showered and sporting too many pregnancy pounds, she knew she wasn't beautiful.

He slipped onto the other side of the bed, looking first at the baby, and then locking eyes with Trish. His lips curled as he reached out and smoothed a hand against her cheek. "You are the most beautiful woman in the world, and I love you."

Funny, when he looked at her that way, she sure felt beautiful.

Closing her eyes, Trish let the warmth from his hand sink in. "I love you, too."

Maybe she drifted off, because the next thing she knew, Tony's voice startled her.

"Why don't you settle in and get some rest? I'll take it from here."

When Trish opened her eyes he was scooping the baby into his arms and lifting her off the bed.

"But there's a mess downstairs." She struggled to keep her eyes open.

"Not anymore." He grinned.

"You cleaned it all?"

"With help. Even the kids, under the direction of Vin, which was like watching a drill sergeant."

Trish chuckled, and leaning forward, snatched a pillow from the end of the bed. "Okay, but just a couple hours. She's going to need to eat."

Tony walked to her side, cradling the baby in one hand, dragging the down comforter over Trish's body with the other. "Sleep tight, beautiful," he said, and then he leaned over, placing a kiss on her forehead.

"And as for you," he said to Angelina as he straightened. "We've got important things to do…like finish off the birthday cake."

Trish shook her head against the pillow. "She's too young for that."

"But Daddy's not." He winked.

Standing there, holding his baby girl, Tony was more striking than he'd ever been. It was hard for Trish to believe she once planned a life without him. Not long ago, all she wanted was a baby who shared her same blood and mysterious genetic code, someone who would fill the loneliness.

Thanks to Tony, Trish got that—and more—because she got him too.

She blew him a kiss as he left the room, and then relaxed her head deeper into the pillow. She'd always imagined a baby would be the key to love like she'd never known, but she was wrong. Angelina was the result of that love.

Tony was the key.

About the Author

Elley Arden is a born and bred Pennsylvanian who has lived as far west as Utah and as far north as Wisconsin. She drinks wine like it's water (a slight exaggeration), prefers a night at the ballpark to a night on the town, and believes almond English toffee is the key to happiness. Elley writes provocative, contemporary, series romance for Crimson Romance. For a complete list of Elley's books visit *http://www.elleyarden.com.*

More from This Author
(From *Crashing the Congressman's Wedding* by Elley Arden)

Alice shoved her feet into rhinestone-studded pumps, checked her teeth for smudges of red lipstick and dashed out the door onto the porch. She had exactly twenty minutes to get to church. Digging into her late mother's beaded clutch, Alice cursed her missing keys and walked as she rummaged, wishing a chat with the mail lady hadn't put her behind schedule.

Ruff. Mouse ran a zigzag pattern across the front yard, brushing filthy fur against her toile skirt.

"Stop it. You're dirty." Alice waved the dog away, but he brushed by again, causing her to stumble and step in a pile of ...

"Crap!" She threw her handbag to the ground and stared at the clump of brown on the tip of her shoe. "Are you serious?" She tossed her head back and roared at the cloudless sky. "You've got to be kidding me."

Stomping her way back to the porch, she kicked off the shoe and scraped the toe in the too-tall grass. Dog doo smashed between the rhinestones. Alice growled, dropped the shoe to the ground and limped into the house, heading straight for her only other pair of remotely matching heels ...character shoes. Wearing beige stage shoes wasn't the fashion statement she hoped to be making today, but she didn't have a choice. She was already late, and the only place to buy shoes in Harmony Falls was the thrift store, which was closed for the congressman's wedding.

These were the moments when Alice missed her mother most. She kissed fingertips and pressed them to Mama's face, smiling at Alice from behind dusty glass. "Tough day, Mama. Wish you were here."

With a frown, Alice hastily fastened the shoes, leaving too much slack. At least the whole day hadn't been a bust. Shirley had delivered mail early on account of the wedding, and in her hand was a letter from the Arts Foundation. Alice's application was a finalist, which put her one step closer to opening an honest-to-God theatre in Harmony Falls. No more *The Sound of Music* in the park pavilion. No more *Peter Pan* in the church social hall. No more Poor Little Alice Cramer, the girl with impossible dreams.

She sighed and then smiled, determined not to let the bad parts of the day drown out the good.

Ten minutes remained, and Alice still had no idea where to find her keys. For all she knew, Mouse stole them again so he could chew on her lucky rabbit's foot. When she rolled her eyes, she noticed her brother's keys hanging on the hook by the door where he'd left them when he rode off with a group of deadbeat friends. Her nose crinkled. Charlie's car smelled like cigarettes and was littered with trash, but it would get her to the church faster than walking.

Snagging the metal off the hook, Alice tiptoed through the grass (careful not to step in anything questionable) and scooped her purse from the front yard before plopping into the driver's seat of Charlie's car.

"Ouch!" She dug a hand underneath yards of scratchy skirt and pulled out a tiara. The glistening crown was pretty. A bit odd, too. And it definitely wasn't hers. She tossed the headpiece into the backseat and shook her head. How Charlie managed to get any woman into this car willingly was beyond Alice. She kicked aside empty paper cups, shut the ashtray, rolled down the windows and pressed pedal to the floor all the way to church.

Making it with a few minutes to spare, Alice paused at the back of the sanctuary, smiling down the lily-lined aisle at the smoking hot man standing before the altar. His tuxedo was tailored, his shoulders were back and his hair was impeccably groomed. He'd worn the same lift to his blond bangs since high school. Back then, the fashionable hair blended with city-bought clothes to make him look even more privileged than he was. Now, almost fifteen years and two professional titles later, the flip of his bangs made her smile, because she recognized it for what it was—who he was—a predictable, responsible, creature of habit.

Alice sighed, smoothed a hand over the snug bodice of her dress and tried to remember a time when she didn't love Justin Mitchell.

He saw her then, and she dug deep into her theatrical bag of tricks to smile with a sincerity that would charm sight-challenged ladies in a theatre's back row. He bought it, smiled back, and Alice imagined the fine lines crinkling around his green eyes. The breath she tried to take stuck in her too-small throat, and she remembered she needed to walk, needed to move, needed to take her place. This wasn't the time for longing or regrets. This was a wedding.

The man she loved was getting married.

But he wasn't marrying her.

Alice released the misery with a shake of her head and then scanned the noisy crowd for friendly faces. Ken and Carole Flemming sat three pews from the altar, three pews too close to the fire, with an empty space between them where Kory should be. Today of all days, Alice missed her best friend, but resident doctors didn't get time off for non-family weddings—even if those weddings featured small-town royalty.

Sucking a mouthful of air, Alice took a step down the aisle. Although she preferred Mrs. Flemming's quiet smile to the rambunctious fawning of just about everyone else in town, for once in her life the attention that went along with a walk down the center aisle wasn't appealing. Alice chose relative anonymity in the back of the church instead.

She slid into the pew and studied the groomsmen, imagining her brother in the mix. Aside from Will and Mark Mitchell, Charlie knew Justin longest; he deserved to be up there, too. She closed her eyes and pictured Charlie cleaned up, with his bow tie tilted and his boutonniere hanging off his lapel. But when she opened her eyes, he wasn't there. Congressman Mitchell couldn't take the risk. Bonds of childhood friendship were no match for the potential embarrassment of having a drunk at the front of the church.

Alice's stomach clenched as she wondered if Charlie was sober today—wherever he was. If not, she prayed he stayed safe and out of too much trouble. She'd been praying for that a lot lately. And she'd keeping praying and hoping it wasn't too late, that Charlie wouldn't end up like their father.

The thoughts tugged acid into Alice's throat, and she held a hand to her mouth. Dropping her shoulders on a heavy exhale, her head followed. Too much emotion for one day. A loose piece of silver thread hung from the bottom of her skirt, and she felt tears that had nothing to do with the thread.

If it weren't for the false eyelashes and extra coats of mascara, she'd have allowed herself a good cry. Justin was getting married, and although she knew this day would come, the finality hit hard.

She sniffed, dabbed beneath her eyes with her knuckles and lifted her head, smile firmly in place. The church teemed with people who had every reason to celebrate. Congressman Justin Mitchell, chief financial officer of Mitchell Company, Inc., was making good on his late father's promise to bring life to this dying town. His congressional term set the stage for tax breaks and corporate-friendly zoning, and his arranged marriage would align the two most powerful families in the state. It didn't hurt that as a wedding present, the bride's uncle promised his new plastics plant to Harmony Falls.

So Alice loved Justin. Big deal. Who was she to stand in the way of progress?

Maisy Carmicheal twisted in her pew. "You look lovely, dear." She smiled at Alice and adjusted her cotton candy pillbox hat. For a beautician, the woman wouldn't know style if it stole her ugly hat and slapped her upside the head. "Wait until you see the bride. Perfection. My best updo ever."

"I'm sure." Alice held her eyes firmly in place despite the urge to let them roll down the aisle. Of course Morgan Parrish was perfect. Her father was the mayor. His power and money made certain she was skinny, educated, and flawless—everything Alice wasn't.

More tears burned the backs of Alice's eyes, but before a drop could fall, a flash of red passed on the Alice's left. Josie Parrish stopped beside Maisy's pew. "The combs aren't holding," she hissed. "Help me, Maisy. This is a disaster. I can't believe she lost that tiara. I told her that bachelorette party was a foolish idea."

Tiara? Hmmm. Alice watched the bride's mother grab Maisy around the wrist and pull her out of the sanctuary. *A tiara.* Like the one Alice sat on in the front seat of Charlie's car? *No.* Alice couldn't imagine Morgan ever stooping low enough to accept a ride from the likes of Charlie. And why would Charlie have been anywhere near Morgan's bachelorette party?

Alice shook her head. The tiara in Charlie's car couldn't be the same tiara Morgan was missing. Besides, after all the years of friendship, Charlie would never hurt Justin.

But a drunk Charlie did things a sober Charlie would never do.

Alice winced. Absolutely not. She refused to believe it. This was just an uncanny coincidence. And yet …how many tiaras were floating around Harmony Falls?

She looked at Justin. He held his hands waist high and alternated squeezing palms, first the right on top and then the left. From the back of the church, she couldn't see him clearly, but she bet he was chewing his bottom lip. He always chewed when he was worried. She couldn't shake the feeling that maybe he had something to chew about.

A few minutes later, Maisy returned to her pew. "Just a little hair snafu, but I worked my magic. The bride is officially breathtaking," she said, gloating loudly enough for several rows to hear.

Alice fidgeted, trying to push thoughts of missing tiaras out of her head. She scratched at her tight bodice, picking at a hard piece of plastic that ran up her side and dug into her right breast. When she did, her elbow bumped the man sitting next to her.

"You look pretty, Alice." The Mitchell's ancient gardener smiled and tipped his hat. "Just like Marilyn Monroe."

"That's sweet, Tubby. Thank you." Never mind that the dress was about as comfortable as a potato sack. She didn't remember it being so itchy when she wore it last year in *Hello, Dolly*. Then again, with no operating budget for her twice-a-year productions, the dress hadn't been dry-cleaned since.

Alice sighed again. Maybe borrowing a dress from the costume closet wasn't the best idea, but her alternatives weren't any better. Wear a frock from the thrift store or drop a bundle on a trip to the city and a dress she'd never wear again. In all honesty, this was hardly the occasion to splurge. She'd have worn black if she thought she could've gotten away with it.

Tubby started humming show tunes under his mint-scented breath, and Alice wondered if he recognized the dress. She slipped down in the pew, wishing she could hold her head up high, wanting just once to attend a Mitchell affair without sitting in the back with the outcasts. But Johnny Cramer made sure his daughter knew her place. Even though he died years before Mama, his words rang clear: "When they look at us, all they see is trash, baby. The sooner you realize it, the better off you'll be."

Yeah? Well, Alice realized it—and she was tired of waiting for the better-off part. All she needed was the grant money, and she'd have a real brick and mortar theatre. She'd know her place then, and everyone else would know her place, too.

Alice Catherine Cramer belonged in the spotlight, not in the audience. She deserved applause, not pity. And with that little pep talk, she smiled, fidgeted again and pressed her back to the uncomfortable pew.

A crinkled hand landed on her leg. "Maybe I'm the only one who thinks it, but that boy's making a mistake." Tubby shook his head. "A man should be happy on his wedding day, and he's not happy."

Alice blinked. Her mouth fell open, and she almost agreed, but before the words tumbled out, trumpets blasted through the church, and Molly Lunsford, cousin of the bride, tossed a handful of rose petals over the white runner near Alice's pew. She looked like a cherub with ringlet curls. The crowd oohed and aahed, and the child bowed. After another handful of petals hit the ground, the little girl sprinted down the aisle toward her papa, where he scooped her into his arms and planted a kiss to her cheek.

Sweet. Alice stole a glance at Justin. Despite the precious child and chuckles from the pews, he was somber, and his misery made her heart hurt. Before she could dwell too much on Justin's lack of happiness, creampuff bridesmaids strolled past, each one stuffier and stiffer than the next. Alice didn't know most of them. They were outsiders, Morgan's friends from a fancy law school in Connecticut, with poufy hair, chandelier earrings and bright pink lips. They looked like the cast of *Willy Wonka* threw up all over the stage.

And then Morgan appeared. The only thing missing was the choir of angels. She was five foot ten with hair of spun silk and a designer dress flown in from France. Whatever the Parrish family had paid for all those layers of lace, they paid too much, Alice thought, smoothing her hand-me-down dress over clenched thighs. She imagined all the overpriced clothes Morgan would buy with the Mitchell family money. What a waste.

The Justin Alice knew wasn't like that. He spent his money, drove new cars, and owned nice homes, but he gave a lot of his money away, and he looked best in blue jeans and a faded Penn State hat with the brim brushing his neck. Morgan wanted to change him, starting with the push to move to D.C. and the "for sale" sign in Justin's front yard. If the banshee got her way, Justin would turn into suit-and-tie-wearing Congressman Mitchell full-time and leave Harmony Falls for good.

As much as the thought depressed Alice, his complete transformation was for the best. When Plain Old Justin was around, Alice couldn't breathe. The lines blurred. He didn't seem so off limits wearing faded jeans and a crooked smile, and she didn't feel so unworthy. In those moments, dreams of being together spilled into her days, and she wasted time walking around a fool in unrequited love.

Thankfully, it'd been a long time since Alice had been stuck in the "I love Justin" rut. She was happy with the direction her life was headed. After today, she hoped the rut would be permanently patched. A girl could dream, couldn't she? Yes, she could. Even if those dreams weren't likely to come true.

A trumpet blast startled Alice as Morgan floated down the aisle with her nose in the air. Alice refused to fawn over a bratty bride, so she focused on the groom instead. His face lengthened and two shadows slashed his cheeks. There wasn't an ounce of joy in the man.

Smile, Justin. Although it would hurt Alice more to see him smile, even the smallest sign of happiness would set her free with the knowledge that at least one of them was getting what they wanted. The idea that he harbored second thoughts pushed her to the edge of the pew.

Smile, Justin. She willed her thoughts over the terrible trumpeting.

But Justin wilted further. There was no shine, no sparkle, no …tiara.

Alice gasped. What if the tiara in Charlie's car was Morgan's? What if they …? She slapped a hand over her mouth. Charlie had been known to romance anything with the right parts, and Morgan's parts were in demand. If Charlie had been drunk, it was possible he made a move.

Oh, God. Alice bit the inside of her cheek. She'd been called a drama queen more times than she could count. Was she being overly dramatic now?

While the Parrish side of the wedding party beamed, the Mitchell side paled. Even Mark, the youngest and goofiest brother, looked worried. And why shouldn't he be? Everything was wrong. This wasn't a wedding march, this was a funeral dirge. The black cloud that appeared over Harmony Falls the day Justin's daddy died had grown into a full-blown storm with Justin directly in its path. And he didn't deserve to be. He was a good man who spent his days helping everybody else. Now it was time for somebody to help him.

The honorable thought carried Alice to her feet. She gulped a few mouthfuls of air, trying to gain courage. "Stop." The shaky command travelled a few pews.

Half the church looked at Alice instead of the bride.

"Can I talk to Justin?" Alice spoke louder this time, pushing out of the pew and into the aisle. "It'll only take a minute. I promise."

Alice hadn't heard so many gasps since she fell off the pavilion stage into the shrubs during opening night of *A Chorus Line.* But she kept her eyes on a gaping Justin, and blocked out the rest.

"Daddy, she's ruining my wedding."

Mayor Parrish stepped in front of his whining daughter and cut off Alice's view of the groom.

Alice stopped cold, watching the mayor move closer. "Justin, I…"

A couple hands wrapped around her upper arms, and Alice felt tugged from behind. "Let's go, little lady. No time for drama. This here ain't a thee-a-ter."

Alice didn't know whose hands were dragging her from the church. Frankly, she didn't care. Her character shoes caught on the runner as Mayor Parrish turned to console his daughter, and that was when Alice saw Justin, his mouth still hanging open.

"She's missing her tiara." Alice looked away from Justin and over the gaping crowd. "Charlie has it." Her voice cracked.

"Get out," Morgan screeched.

The next thing Alice knew, heavy doors shut in her face and Gilbert Hoover plopped her on a cement step. "Go home, little lady. Fix yourself some tea. It'll be all right. You'll see."

What did Gilbert know about all right? He pumped gas for a living. He lived in a doublewide. The pancake breakfast was his idea of gourmet "eats." This town was mad, and she was neck-deep in their insanity. Well, no more. It might be honorable to help a man who was making a terrible mistake, but from now on, Alice Cramer was only helping herself.

Justin could marry the banshee. Alice was going home. She lifted her skirt and stomped barefoot down the church steps.

"Where're your shoes?" Gilbert called.

It seemed her dignity wasn't the only thing Alice left lying in the aisle.

• • •

Justin stared at his beet-red bride-to-be as she cowered in her father's arms. Strands of inky silk slid from her hair combs and stuck to her wet cheeks. "What's going on?"

She burrowed deeper into her father's chest. "Alice is crazy."

Maybe. Charlie's little sister had done a lot of crazy things in her life, but standing up in church without good reason seemed extreme, even for a Cramer.

Between Morgan's sniffles, Justin could've heard a boutonniere pin drop in the stricken church. He glanced at his mother, sitting stoically in the front pew. No doubt she figured he had a plan to get the situation under control. But for the first time since his father died, leaving the job of diplomacy to him, Justin was at a loss for words.

He should probably start with an apology to his mother and permit her the *'I-told-you-so.'* She'd warned him time and time again about the damage Charlie could do to his reputation. He glanced at Morgan, picturing her missing tiara sitting atop her head. Apparently she didn't get the same lecture.

Sickness swirled in Justin's stomach, and a flash interrupted his speculative trance. The bright light drew his attention down the aisle to a large man with an even larger camera taking photos of the twirling flower girl. At least someone was having fun. But as soon as the sarcastic thought faded, another more ominous thought formed. That man, that camera, could ruin Justin by capturing an unsavory, unscripted moment and putting it on display.

Justin's chest clenched. He had a choice to make. He could either go through with what he once thought of as a politically advantageous wedding solely to save face and as a result, risk life with a duplicitous woman, or he could step back, take a breather and make certain he was doing the right thing by marrying a woman he didn't trust and didn't love simply to follow through on his father's promise.

With an inhale and an exhale, Justin raised his hands. "I need a minute."

"Don't you dare walk out on me," Morgan threatened through clenched teeth.

He hadn't thought about walking out until she suggested it, and now that she had, he wanted to. Walking wouldn't solve the big problem, but if he walked, nobody would see him blow. And for the first time in years, he heard the ticking of a time bomb with each beat of his heart.

Months' worth of frustration trapped between his cummerbund and bowtie. He'd allowed himself to be a pawn in a game his father started years ago. There were no more clandestine whiskey and cigar meetings between Marvin Mitchell and Robert Parrish, but their plans for power remained. If their dreams for political dominance had died along with Justin's father, Justin wouldn't be standing here today. But he was standing here, a willing accomplice, because as Marvin's oldest son, it was his duty to follow through with his father's best-laid plans, plans which included a Congressional seat and a loveless marriage.

Crazy? Maybe. But his father said powerful families arranged marriages all the time. They were business transactions of mutual benefit. In this case, Justin would get a beautiful, poised, politically-appropriate wife, who happened to come with a dowry of several hundred million dollars in the shape of an international plastics plant, and Morgan would get a wealthy husband with power, influence and title. Everybody won, unless, of course, you counted love, which Justin didn't. Love didn't win elections. Love didn't balance the measly budgets of rural Pennsylvania towns. Love was one of the few luxuries powerful people couldn't afford.

Or so he'd been told over and over again by the most unlikely source, his bride-to-be. He'd been focused and methodical about marrying Morgan for the power and stability her family could offer this town, and yet he stood here, shaken by the unknown. Was it possible Morgan had risked his reputation and all they planned to accomplish together by carrying on with Charlie?

When Justin looked at Morgan, she looked away.

On the first wave of impulse Justin had permitted in years, he threw up his hands. "I apologize, but this isn't going to happen today."

"I'll kill her," Morgan roared. So much for poise under pressure.

Any other time, Justin would've placated her for the sake of keeping appearances, but now he simply wanted to get away. He walked up the aisle with gasps and gossip to his back. He could only imagine his mother's fear and confusion. It was almost enough to turn him around. Almost.

"When I get my hands on that little …" Morgan's threats against Alice faded and somewhere in the distance a door slammed.

Justin didn't stop to see what happened. At the moment, he was too numb to care. His mind warned that this could be political suicide, but he needed the truth. Once he knew what Alice knew, he could form a plan.

He reached down to scoop up the pair of shoes that littered the aisle. Alice Cramer had given him grief since the day they first met. She had better have a damn good explanation now.

Also check out *Change My Mind*
and *Save My Soul* from Elley Arden.
In the mood for more Crimson Romance?
Check out *Simple Gone South* by Alicia Pace Hunter at
CrimsonRomance.com.